RANGE

Do Phleadan.
Gach Aua.

Joe Byrne

Realhna 2000

To the memory of Mary Jo Foran

FREE RANGE

RANGE

John F. Deane

WOLFHOUND PRESS

First published 1994 by
WOLFHOUND PRSS Ltd
68 Mountjoy Square
Dublin 1

Wolfhound Press receives financial assistance from the Arts Council/An Chomhairle Ealaíon, Dublin.

British Library Cataloguing in Publication Data
A catalogue record for this book is available from the British Library.

ISBN 0-86327-430-7

ACKNOWLEDGMENTS:
Some of these stories were published in *Stet, The Sunday Tribune, The Achill Island Book, The Honest Ulsterman, A Page Falls Open* and broadcast on RTE Radio; several stories have been shortlisted for the Francis MacManus Award and the Hennessy / Cognac Award.

Cover design: Joe Gervin
Cover illustration: Katharine White
Typesetting: Wolfhound Press
Printed in the Republic of Ireland by Colour Books, Dublin

Contents

THE WIDOW, ELLIE CLAINE

The first stroke was a gentle tap on the shoulder, a gift, as if someone who had been following her about for days had finally whispered a warning in her ears, and had gone away. It left a weight dragging against the left side of her body, a tick under the left eye, a slight drawing-down of the left side of her mouth, slurring her speech; perhaps, too, there was a diminution of strength in her left wrist, a barely perceptible stiffening of the muscles in her left leg. But all of that, her family considered, could as easily be put down to old age as to a stroke. As if they did not believe the evidence her body presented to them, as if she were guilty of some deceit; imagine! How strange people are, especially those whom you think you know best of all! Exercise, the doctor said, gentle exercise, to keep the blood active in its courses through the body.

She took to walking the road in front of her house, once up to the top of the hill, then down again, past her own gate, on as far as the turn into Dogrose Lane, and back to stand a while at the gate before going indoors. Four or five hundred yards, all told, on a country road not marked on any tourist's map, a road that had no existence now other than its featuring in the geography of her blood.

She knew there could be very little time left to her. She was almost ... yes, 'happy' could be the word; she was becoming light, and every object about the house was growing dense, sodden, unwieldy; something in her becoming birdsong, thistledown, echo, though the body adhered as much as ever, dragging her every which way. Perhaps, she thought, the real meaning of a word, like *love*, like *memory*, like *death*, waits far beyond the word itself, a truth glimpsed sometimes, but never held. She was little more now than six stone, lighter than she had been for ... oh for some sixty years at least! And still the burden of the body was as wearisome as ever, thwarting her, keeping her down, listing her now like an old boat.

Declan was being so good to her, too, and even Elizabeth. The children behaved, they were quiet and considerate, and all of them so perfectly tactful. But what she wished for during those days was that the children should be brash and noisy, clamouring as they used to for the box of biscuits on top of the dresser, or asking to be allowed to watch the cartoons on TV. All that boisterous, shrill youthfulness, they were suppressing it for her sake, but she wanted to feel the jangling bones of the old red house that once again had the riot of children within its walls. There was no time left for lies.

The children drew back from her now when she jerked towards them, to ruffle Allison's hair, to break open Kenneth's biscuit so she could watch him lick the cream from between the halves. Then, when she spoke, trying to show them how much she felt for them, their eyes would be drawn to the trickles of saliva that escaped from the left side of her mouth. When she had urged Declan and Elizabeth to go off out and enjoy themselves and she would only be too glad to look after the children, how had she bunged that up too? Elizabeth, God bless her, always tetchy, bridled, as if they had been irking her by their presence and their kindness, as if she had been envying them their youth and vitality, and envying them, above all, their future. How irritating now that her words could not keep pace with her thoughts, with this new life tiding into forgotten inlets of her being; a joy manifesting itself in spittle from the side of her mouth, in jerks of hoarse laughter that pained her chest, in embarrassing rumbles from her stomach.

All those summer days the swifts were skimming along the surfaces of air, their sharp, tin-edged screeches like the cries of children at the sea's shore. They swooped and levelled with an exuberance she had not noticed before, from early morning until the last flitches of warm, evening light. Then the bats took over, swooping and levelling too, but with a tangible silence all about them. Even the bats she came to love, swift and bat filling day and night with their living and slaughtering. The swifts would be leaving soon, and she would not see them again. She tried to separate them into families, the elders and the youngsters, into individuals she could name and whose movements she might trace, but they made such a tangled net across the sky that she had to resign that task almost at once.

The hedgerows were swollen with late summer life: cow-parsley, knapweed, the trailing azure flowers of the vetch, the delicate pink of the bramble blossom. There was wild thyme, too, and wild mint, a kitchen garden offering riches far greater than the ... what, 30? ... years of bits and bobs, letters and notices and cards that she had shoved into drawers and boxes since Edward's death. The blackthorn bushes already had their stores of hard green sloes, small and bitter yet like the beads on her rosary; soon they would be turning black, and then that soft blue flush would come over them to tell they were ripe for the picking. She would not be there, she knew, for that virgin blush.

Down the hill as far as the turn into Dogrose Lane. Some-times, in Harte's field, the hares would be busy, big fellows, tetchy before the rising in the distance of the rumour of an engine, or the barking of a dog. Towards her they seemed indifferent and she could pause and watch their movements among the riches of the aftergrass. The pheasants, too, in the bushes beyond the field, called and jumped and flew their little flights. Once a male, cock-of-the-hoop and law-di-daw, crossed the road in front of her so that she began to wonder if she had taken on already some beginnings of invisibility. She stamped her foot hard on the road, and the pheasant gave a short, indignant leap, flung her a disdainful glance before resuming his sangfroid and continuing on his way.

The summer days passed; Declan came and went, and neighbours sometimes called. They worried about her, but what could they do? She insisted she was managing quite well. No she did *not* want to go into hospital; she was terrified of the loss of independence, of being fed bedpans and platitudes and wet-blotting-paper hospital food. Declan was going to arrange a home help, she would think about that. She thought of having the phone taken out; but that would not be fair on them, not fair at all.

Some nights now, in late August, the darkness was so deep before she slept that her old fear and lonesomeness rose again like mists she could almost touch. She had been sleeping alone, in that room and in that bed, for thirty-eight years, since Edward, about to bring the tractor down to the shed on Dogrose Lane, had had his awful accident. Darkness in the country night can be dark beyond darkness and she was not sleeping well now, as if the body had had all the rest it ever wanted, or as if the spirit were in rehearsal for perpetual wakefulness.

August turned to September, her fingers were dried leaves, ready to fall. On the first Friday of that month, in the warm afternoon, she climbed the stairs to her room. Declan and Elizabeth, without the children, would come by evening. She dreaded the fuss and the untruth of their arrival, Declan quizzing her about how well she was caring for herself, Elizabeth's poorly concealed disquiet about the dust, the floor, the windows ... She filled the delft-ware basin on her dressing-table with cold water; she would sponge her body into some semblance of freshness. As she undressed she grew curious again about the whiteness of her body, with all those veins standing out in shades of blue and purple. She stood naked before the mirror. She gazed at that small, yellow-white, shrivelling body, somehow unfamiliar to her in these years, so other to that full, desired body that had been lost somewhere in the labyrinth of the years.

That was the moment when she was stricken again. The left side of her body simply ceased to function and she heeled over like a felled tree. There had been a short pain, razor-sharp and hot, and it had passed at once, leaving her stretched on the floor, shivering with an extraordinary happiness. Her mind had come fully and vividly alert, so that even the texture of the planks of the bedroom floor fascinated her. She heard a bluebottle flinging itself against the window of the room; she was convinced that she could hear the water lying in the basin. At once she knew that it could not be this way, it would not be right for them to find her so, the image left to him would sear Declan through for ever. She felt, rather than heard, someone on the road outside, coming up the hill from Dogrose Lane, approaching the gate of the old, red house.

She managed to roll herself onto her right side, then onto her back; she raised her right arm sufficiently to draw her nightdress from the bed. It was her favourite, a gentle pink with dream-flowers in blue across the breast. She heard the rusty, heavy squeal of the gate being opened, and closed, and the dull clang of the hasp coming down. Heavy footsteps sounded on the gravel towards her front door. Too soon, too soon. She worked feverishly, pulling her nightdress along the floor towards her, pulling herself to meet it. She got her head in, then her right arm worked itself in along the sleeve.

She squirmed, like an earth-creature, working her way in, but her left side did not respond at all, her left arm hung loose and dead and dragging. Again she rolled herself onto her front and worked the nightie down her body. Her heart thudded within her ... or was that a knocking at her front door? No, not knocking; she heard the latch lifted, the scrape of the opening door along the linoleum, the latch dropped again. There was someone in the hall below.

She must raise herself onto the bed. She worked herself onto her right knee, her left side against the side of the bed. It was in that lifeless side of her body that the heart pounded and drove, causing no pain, but urging a mildly exciting current through her body. The footsteps had crossed the kitchen floor beneath the room and now they were on the stairs. There was that old, familiar creak of the third step as a heavy weight was placed on it. One, last, effort.

She rose, on her right leg, teetered a moment, like an old factory chimney that had been exploded at the base, poised before the fall. That view from her window, the garden, the hedge, the ash tree, and then the lumps and wastes of the valley; that golden and silver light over it all; what truths there were out there, and what lies flourishing amongst them! The footsteps were on the landing, outside her door. She let her body fall onto the bed. It was all right now, she was ready. The latch lifted on the bedroom door. She was breathing with great difficulty – quick, searching gasps; her heart was thundering within her, a great irregular hammering on a bass drum, the skin tightened across her chest. The door opened.

Edward closed the door softly behind him.

'Sorry, love,' he said. 'I had some difficulty with the Fordson. But it's all settled up now, right as rain.'

He washed his hands and face in the water in the delft basin. He undressed, and then he was on the bed beside her, fondling her breasts, her nipples rising to his touch and oh that easy, delicate expertise of his as he kissed her, rousing her to a need of him before he entered her. And then she was gripping him about the shoulders, running her hands along his back as he brought her quickly, certainly, to a perfect and uncontrollable climax.

THE WET FINGER

Adrian was writing his letter to the Christmas Angel. It was only mid-November but he knew that the letter would have a great distance to travel, over land and lands, over rivers and oceans, through the air, across endless deserts of frozen snow; then, from the North Pole, straight up on the draught of angels' wings into the heavens until it passed through the skin of the ordinary world into the workshops of eternity.

' ... and if possible a Meccano set, so I can build machines and motors that really work. And yes I heard your carriage last year; I could hear the tinkling of the bells, it was near midnight and I was still awake, with the excitement, it was a sky bright from the moon and still and very cold; I heard the tinkling, and I looked out, but I saw nothing. I didn't sleep for a long time after that, with the excitement, and then I thought that you weren't going to come because I wasn't asleep and because I might see you. But why you don't want me to see you I don't understand; I'd love to see you, and I wouldn't tell, truly I wouldn't. But maybe it was on your way back you came here. Anyway, thanks for the things you gave me last year. Con Connors says that the bells I heard were only the bells of old Andy Cronin's bike and that he was swaying across the road on his way home from Lynott's pub. But I know they were the bells on your carriage as you went over the island on your way ... '

Adrian sealed the envelope and addressed it. He felt good. He slept well.

On his way to school next morning he bought a stamp, promising himself that he would post the letter in the small green box fitted into the wall of MacHenry's General Store, first thing the following Monday morning. At school, during big break, he mentioned the letter to Aengus, his special friend.

'When you post the letter it goes to Dublin, and from there some of the worker angels take it all the way to the North Pole. Then they gather up all the letters that have come in from all over the world, carry them up on their wings into Heaven, and other angels help the Christmas Angel to do the work, and to get the toys ready for Christmas Eve.'

Con Connors was peeling the bark off a rhododendron bush and he overheard their conversation. Con was small and stocky; his father cut his hair by placing a porridge bowl over Con's head and cutting everything tight against his skull, right up to the edge of the bowl. This made Con look like a mastiff; indeed the squat power of his body added to this impression of ferociousness; he was rough, belligerent, quick; they had nicknamed him 'the Dog'.

'So!' he said to Adrian, 'you still believe in the Christmas Angel? And I suppose you believe in other angels, too?'

'Of course I do,' Adrian answered.

'You're a right eejit, then; everybody knows there's no such thing as angels.'

'There are so angels!' Adrian answered. 'Isn't it the archangel Michael who's the guardian of our island? And wasn't it an angel brought the news to Mary that she was going to have a baby? And wasn't it angels who came to Jesus when he was in his agony in the garden? And don't we all have a guardian angel beside us all the time, to help us and to keep us safe?'

'You awful eejit!' said the Dog. 'So you tell me there's an angel there beside you right now keeping you safe?'

'Yes, of course there is.'

'Well, OK then, let's see if your angel will mind you.'

The Dog put the index finger of his right hand into his mouth and wet it, then reached and rubbed the finger down along Adrian's cheek.

'There you are!' the Dog shouted. 'Now I've laid the wet finger on you and you're a coward if you don't fight. We'll see if your angel will help you now. Let's see the proof!'

'I don't want to fight you,' Adrian replied, his stomach already beginning to heave within him. 'You're a lot bigger than me, and you're older, and it wouldn't be fair. And anyway it's not something to be fighting about.'

'You're chicken, that's all, you're just chicken. And it proves you don't really believe in angels. You're chicken. And I bet you eat a lot of chicken liver. And chicken wings. They'll help you to fly like one of your stupid angels. Chicken, chicken, chicken!'

During the rest of the day Adrian sat quietly in his desk. The other boys knew about the challenge. They were hoping there would be a fight out on the road after school. Adrian was small, too, and thin, not built to fight the Dog. It would be a massacre, and that would be great to watch.

Three o'clock came and the final prayers of the day were said. The boys were out the door before the *Amen* had died away. Adrian was slow getting his things together. The Dog had gone out. When he left the schoolroom Adrian decided he would go to the toilets at the back of the yard. There he unbuttoned his trousers and sat down on one of the wooden seats and waited.

He was scared, very scared. He had been in fights before, but they were short and not very serious. The Dog revelled in violence. Adrian was hoping the boys would get tired waiting, and go home. He could not leave it too late, however, for it would be getting dark and the lane up from school to the main road passed between high hedges of rhododendron bushes; they could be filled with those terrifying beings that live in and feed off the darkness.

When he did come out there was no sign of any of the boys on the lane. He hung his bag on his back so that he could hold his trousers up. He was still in short trousers, and he wore braces; he was not yet able to button the braces at the back. Soon, he hoped, soon he would be able to get into long trousers, like the others, like the Dog, like Aengus, and be able to wear a belt, one of those coloured ones with the silver buckle shaped like an S. That would prove he wasn't a child any longer.

For the moment he had to walk cautiously, gripping his trousers. He was nearing the gate; the boys seemed to have gone home. He came out onto the road and suddenly several of them jumped out from behind the wall; they were laughing loudly. The Dog was with them, grim, ugly and determined.

'Right, the angel Gabriel, let's see what you can do now,' said the Dog, and he came up to Adrian, wet his finger once more and rubbed it down along Adrian's cheek. 'You can't deny the wet finger, you have to fight.'

'I can't fight now,' Adrian answered, 'can't you see I'm late and they'll be waiting for me at home.'

'You're chicken, then, just chicken, that's what you are. And it proves that I'm right; there are no angels, you've admitted it. And some day, wait and see, I'll get you, and I'll break you into little pieces. So there!'

Adrian began to cry, though he was trying his very best not to; all the other boys were jeering and taunting him, even Aengus, even some of the tiny ones out of lower and higher infants; he began to run, holding up his trousers with one hand, brushing the other against his face to wipe away the tears. The Dog noticed the trousers and he sent a whirlwind of hoots and laughter after him; someone threw a stone and it bounded along the road near him. He ran the half mile home, then crept upstairs to the bathroom to wash the day from his face.

That evening a storm came in over the island. The winds were noisy ghosts rushing through the trees around the house, waves broke over the tiny harbour wall so violently it seemed as if wall and pier and curraghs could lift away over the sea like great, black rooks; the darkness was filled with a lank, cold rain. Suddenly all the lights went out. Candles were found, and lit, and an old lamp was filled with paraffin oil, the globe rubbed clean, the wick trimmed, and the kitchen filled with a delicate, white light. Shadows grew enormous, shifting over the walls. For the first time in months the family sat together, telling stories, hushing the storms about them.

Adrian carried his candle with him upstairs to bed. He watched his shadow go up before him, small at first, flat on the steps, then enlarging until it topped the stairs and began to move up the wall where it became immense, distorted and terrifying; then, as he came towards his bedroom it shrank again, touching the knob of the door at the same moment he did. In his room, as he said his night prayers, there was a gentle light, small but certain; 'Oh angel of God my guardian dear to whom God's love commits me here ... ' He lay awake for a long time, thinking, watching the shadows shift with whatever breeze caressed the small, white flame. 'Ever this night be at my side, to light and guard, to ... ' Adrian was suddenly ashamed of his cowardice; of course there were angels, ruling and guiding. He would not be afraid of shadows; he felt no fear of the darkness that came as he blew the candle out. He made his decisions and curled down to sleep.

Next day, at big break, before anyone could say a word to him, he went up to Con, the Dog, put his index finger in his mouth, wet it, and brought it down across Con's face.

'That's to prove there's angels,' he said, 'and spirits, and ghosts, and there's an angel beside you, too, a lovely angel, trying to love you and keep you, and he's ready to be with you for all of your life, even though he might have a hard job in front of him.'

The Dog was taken aback and could think of nothing to say; instead he pushed Adrian roughly in the chest and made him stagger backwards. Then he grinned, put his big fists into his pockets and walked away, whistling.

At three o'clock the boys went rushing up the lane. Adrian's stomach churned inside him; he felt he could still run away from it all, he thought he might even get sick with fear. Con the Dog was waiting, his jacket off, his bag thrown on the ground, his sleeves rolled up, his face screwed into a leer of anticipation. Adrian came into the ring of boys, and there was nobody to stand up for him. He took off his bag and gave it to Aengus who took it, reluctantly, watching the others for their reaction. Adrian took off his jacket and handed it to Aengus. He turned to face the Dog.

'Right,' said the Dog, as he began to prance about, his fists already striking at the air, 'right then, let's see these angels of yours in action.'

Adrian raised his two hands and made fists of them, small, white fists. The Dog ran at him, fists flailing like windmills. Adrian put his hands up before his face to save himself, but the fists hit him again and again, on the head, on the nose, on the mouth. The Dog punched him hard in the stomach and he felt all his breath leap out of him into the November air. He staggered backwards and the ring of boys opened to let him through. He fell onto the grass at the edge of the road. The Dog stood laughing above him, there seemed to be boys everywhere, mocking, leering, shouting with delight.

'Get up, you yellow chicken you!' shouted the Dog. 'Get up, and take what's coming to you! My God but I'm going to blacken you, I'll flatten you, I'll thicken you, I'll rip you into little pieces. Get up, you rotten yellow chicken, get up!'

The Dog was king, leaping and twirling, striking at cowed, imaginary shapes in the air, bowing and posturing, leading his powerfilled dance.

Adrian scrambled to his feet; the Dog backed a little from

him onto the gravelly space before the gate; Adrian put his head down and lunged, hitting him squarely in the stomach. The Dog gasped and fell, Adrian falling on top of him. The Dog wrestled him over onto the gravel, now Adrian was underneath and the Dog got himself up onto Adrian's chest and sat on him.

'You dirty coward!' he shouted down at him, 'that was a rotten trick!' and he began to pummel Adrian's face from his position on his chest. All Adrian could do was to keep his hands before his face but the blows fell all over him, sending waves of hurt through his face to break behind his eyes and forehead.

'Let him up! Let him up!' the boys were screaming at the Dog. The Dog rose slowly, then kicked Adrian hard in the ribs as he left him. The boys went silent when they saw that and the Dog glanced at them, hesitant. Adrian could feel the blood coming from his nose and he reached a hand into his pocket for a handkerchief as he struggled to his feet. The Dog lurched at him again at that moment and landed a punch to his stomach that doubled him up in pain. Then the Dog brought his knee up into the younger boy's face. This was too much for the boys and some of them cried 'Shame!' and booed at the Dog.

Now nobody has ever outlined the rules for a fight such as this; there is no final bell, there are no rounds, there is no time limit, no final whistle. There are no boundary lines, no referee. Adrian was crying and bleeding and gasping for breath as he knelt on the gravel; the Dog was walking away sullenly, muttering 'I knew he was chicken' but he got no response from the others. Adrian got up again. He came slowly after the Dog, tapped him on the shoulder, then stood back with his fists raised.

'It's over,' the Dog said, 'you're beaten. Go home.'

Adrian swung his fist at him, the Dog stepped aside easily and Adrian staggered forward. He turned and came back; he could scarcely see through his tears but once again he flung his fists at the Dog's face, missing him completely.

'Stop!' said the Dog. 'Can't you see it's over? I'll only kill you can't you see?'

Adrian landed a fist on the Dog's nose, a hard thump that sent a feeling of satisfaction through his whole body. The Dog howled, holding his face, and Adrian charged. The Dog stepped aside and as Adrian staggered past him he put out his leg and tripped him; he fell flat on his face on the gravel. Now the Dog lost control, he leaped onto Adrian's back and thumped at the back of his head and his shoulders wildly. It was Aengus who jumped forward and grabbed the Dog to pull him off, shouting 'Stop! that's not fair, get off, it's you who's the chicken'; several other boys joined him in dragging the Dog away.

Adrian began to gather himself off the ground again. His knees were cut, his clothes filthy, one of his eyes was almost closed. He shook his head, looking for the Dog.

'Where is he?' he shouted, 'where is he gone?'

The Dog had turned away to look for his bag and jacket; he began to walk home, alone, and quiet.

'Come back, come back here until the fight is over,' Adrian shouted after him. He stumbled towards the Dog once more, teetering about as if drunk. As he came close he called out:

'Turn around and face me. The fight is not over yet.'

Con stopped, turned, and faced him. Adrian put his fists up and lunged. Con simply held his hand out and kept Adrian at bay; then he pushed, and Adrian stumbled backwards again. Con turned for home. But the younger boy kept following until at last Con said, very quietly, but loudly enough for those boys who had followed to hear:

'OK, the fight is over; you're not chicken, OK? the fight is over. I won't fight you again.'

Adrian stopped dead, looking at him. At once all the strength left in his body flooded out of him and he sat down heavily on the road. Con turned and walked home. Aengus came up with Adrian's bag and jacket and, as he helped him on with the coat he clapped him proudly on the back. It was over.

The afternoon was already turning dark; at home, Adrian knew, the fire would be lit by now and the lights would be on in the kitchen. His mother would have begun the evening meal and there would be a scent of goodness filling the whole house. He must ask her, this evening, to buy him a long trousers, and a belt. And that letter he had written ... perhaps he would not post it now after all.

ALAS, POOR FRANKIE

Francis Patrick Hanrahan had never heard of such a thing: a pipe band! to come ranting through his graveyard to honour the memory of the senator! All that wind, the noise that would swell like a great balloon and burst into little spits of nothing! The crowds would come trampling all over the poor un-notables lying about, whose only wish was to lie quietly in their beds and have a few thin montbretia blowing over them. A pipe band in a graveyard! talk about waking the dead! and who else but the living devil inside him would have persuaded Canon McHugh to allow such a thing? Francis Patrick Hanrahan, 'Frankie' to his friends, lifted his pick-axe in a quick surge of petulance and brought it biting down on Michael the Twin O'Hara's chest. The pick struck deep into summer-hardened clay.

'Oh God, I'm sorry, Michael, I am truly sorry, but you know well I don't mean you any disrespect at all. No, no, not at all, not at all.'

There was no answer. Frankie was crestfallen.

'Now, Canon, look what you've made me do.'

But the thick daub on O'Hara's grave had cracked under the blow; Frankie found it easier to fork and spade the rest of it, with a generous additional supply of peat moss, into reasonably friable clay, and he spread it all out neatly over the surface of the grave. O'Hara father, grandfather, grandmother, greatgrandmother, greatgrandfather ... they'd all be chuffed even though the crowd, jostling for position round the senator's grave, would pass them by without as much as a peep. Frankie trudged off to the north-eastern corner of the graveyard and lifted a wreath of fresh flowers from the senator's grave.

'Sorry, yer honour, but you'll no doubt be getting a whole scatter of flowers this afternoon and there's been nobody nigh the O'Haras for five years back; poor Mrs herself will be joining them all soon enough.'

Only a haughty silence lifted and hung over the senator's plot.

Frankie left the flowers on the O'Hara grave and went back to the south-west corner of the graveyard, a hidden corner near the side door to the sacristy. He had gone down barely three feet yet for Sally O'Malley's grave. To pick and shovel out a seven-foot deep grave wasn't getting any easier; he had to do the job now in slow stages, one foot at a time, or a little more if the soil was dry, then off to do a bit of scything or weeding, or to boil up a teapotful of tea, or even do murder to a bottle of Guinness kept cool in the water-butt by the sacristy door. Back to do another foot or two, until he was fairly sure that he'd get the job finished in advance of the arrival.

The mid-morning sun was hot. There had been no rain now for days, weeks even. The countryside, and even the people, seemed to have swollen into a state of tetchiness that made everything dry and rough to the touch. The heat must have got to Sally in the end. God but I'll bet she's glad to have missed the senator's piping! a class of a socialist or a communist or something she was; couldn't stand the Fianna thisses and the Fianna thatses, with their words that were noisy belches and their promises that were candle-flames offered to a western gale; jobs for the boys, that's all, she'd say; and now a pipe band for one of the boys, she'd have leaped ten feet out of her grave if she'd been in her grave.

Frankie chuckled loudly as he went on digging. And look!

she was to be buried in her darling daughter's grave, right up against the wall of the chapel she never set foot in during her adult life. A fine woman, Sally, a fine woman, true and faithful to the very last. The Canon would get his own back now, and what could poor Sally do about it? they'd put her down among the Fianners and the Catholics and the murmuring hypocrites and her only request was that her shrivelled body be given the dignity of the fire, that her ashes be put into a thimble and the thimbleful be cast onto the air from the highest point on the Cathedral Cliffs. She would float out and away, like the wild geese after winter, out over the free and tumbling waves of the Atlantic Ocean. Poor Sally, not here you won't, not with the Canon still running the show after all of these years; remember those words, Sally? 'resurrection of the body, remember? and life everlasting. Amen!'

On Monday morning Mrs Furlong had come in, the last to go into the Furlong plot, that's for sure. A right boatload of the Furlongs in there now, jolly for them, a fine old party even though several of them hadn't got along too well together in this life. Poor old Sally now, with only little Sheila, and poor Sheila never got too far into this life before she had to leave it again. Poor Sheila, poor, poor Sally.

Frankie went off to check the Furlong plot; he patted the fresh mound on Nell's grave to keep it neat and shapely, and rearranged some of the flowers that were already beginning to wilt in the heat. He took worn-out stems of flowers from the Claine plot and the Maguire plot, and wheelbarrowed them over to the waste patch at the furthest corner — the north-west frontier he called it — of the graveyard. He threw them onto the pile of old branches — dried-up grasses, plastic bowls with their plastic wreathes, all the withered stalks and leaves and rubbish from a busy graveyard life. Have to put a match to that, one of the days; but better not right now, with the pipers and the notables all puffing their way about; the smoke might get them, choke them to blazes, the pipers getting the senator's notes out wrong. Love to do it! hah! but there's that old Canon now would love the chance to fling me out onto the road, bring in the JCB he would, too, and that's me gone for sure. Th'oul' whure!

'Yez'd all miss me now, wouldn't ye?' he called out.

A general murmur of assent rose from the grasses and montbretia, the fuchsia and the purple loosestrife and from the tall and silent yew-trees in their clusters.

A sudden snorting lurch of clay beneath his feet startled him.

'Oh God, Tom, I'm sorry; I wasn't thinking. There y'are now, I've walked on your stomach again. But then you won't let me tidy you up a bit so that I'll know where you are and not walk on you. I never knew a man wanted so much to lie low and unnoticed as yourself, Tom, a man after me own heart, of course, though, don't you know? What's that? Whure? Me a whure? Oh, the Canon; yes, yes, yes, I know you can't call a man a whure. But then again why not? Doesn't he sell himself away all the time, too? His big car an' his bullying the lesser folk, and his freezer full of steaks an' all to that? An' you, Tom, you better watch your stomach this afternoon for the senator's lot will be quick enough to stamp on your stomach and your face and your balls, just you watch out now, Tom, you watch out!'

Frankie chuckled loudly, a chuckle that turned too quickly to a wheeze, the wheeze into a harsh and grating bout of coughing that brought him to his knees on the gravel path. He coughed and retched drily until his elbows were on the gravel and he was crouched in agony, tears coming down his face. Oh Jesus Christ, me oul' true friend, when are you goin' to come an' give me a bit o' peace? Oh Canon MacHugh, you whure you, you walkin', whistlin' whure!

He sat for a while on the low stone surround of O'Meara's plot: one of the best kept plots of them all, nasturtiums and roses and antirrhinums. How did they manage to water them all, from below, I mean? Weeding, yes, you can figure out how they do that, after all they're close to the roots, but watering? and they never asked Frankie to do the job; considerate, that, to a seventy-year-old. Thank ye kindly but ye know I'd do it willin' and without the askin' but the windy oul' whure says we must go easy on the water these days, the weather you know. And then again didn't he throw a fine sup himself on the senator's spot this morning? Oh! but ye can't take for gospel every word that comes pebblin' out of his oul' snout!

Frankie finished digging Sally's grave and found the almost perfect skull he had expected to find. A small, too-white skull, and crushed about the right temple. Ah, poor Sheila, God help her, the poor wee child. He climbed out of the grave, tidied up the waiting mound of soil and laid the artificial grass over the hole. Time for lunch, Sheila, come on love, join us in a bite. His bicycle rested against the sacristy wall; he took the bag from the carrier and went back to sit by Sally's grave. He put Sheila's skull on the mound of soil and he sat down on the low flat tombstone of the O'Rorke's. Never get a word out of the O'Rorkes; maybe they're all just too haughty for the likes of me. The flat o' me arse to ye, then, if that's the case. Tomato sandwiches. No, he couldn't face them; no hunger in him any more, not for weeks now. He got up again and fetched his bottle of Guinness from the barrel of rain-water outside the sacristy door.

Frankie took a quick gulp. Almost at once he was retching again, a great wasp-sting of pain screaming from the hummock of his chest and finishing as a thudding, knocking dullness against the insides of his temples. He bent his head down between his knees, the sweat dripping from him though he was trembling with the cold. The bottle slipped from his fingers and the black liquid began to spill out in a frothing pool onto the grass. He moved quickly to save the drink and the moment passed.

'Ah Sheila, love, when a man can no longer hold a little mouthful o' Guinness it's time he was allowed in to share all the little pleasures of his long-gone friends. I've been having this hankering to do a spot of visiting, don't ye know; there's so many up there in Mount Jerome in Dublin, and there's Glasnevin with all its famous people, and I've heard tell that Montparnasse in Paris is a gem; and Montmartre, too, they tell me; meself and yerself and our own wee Sally, now, wouldn't it be great for the three of us to go visiting in Paris? We'd have the rare old time of it up there in Montparnasse.'

As soon as he felt a little strength and steadiness return to his body, Frankie picked Sheila up from the mound and put her, together with his untouched sandwich and the remains of the bottle, into the bag on the carrier of his bike. He was sitting, half a-doze, half alive, on the O'Rorke slab when Canon MacHugh came out the sacristy door. The Canon was a small man with a pinched face, heavy-rimmed glasses, and a few strands of white hair carefully carpeting as much as they could of his ringed, bald head.

'Mr Hanrahan!' he called several times before Frankie was aware of him.

'Ah, Canon, it's yerself. So I'm still in it after all!'

'Yes, Francis Patrick, it's me, and yes you're still in it. It's after two o'clock. Did you clip the grass around the back of the senator's grave as I asked you to? They'll be arriving shortly now, you know.'

'O God, Canon, I forgot that. I was digging the grave here for poor Sally who'll be with us in the morning and I forgot all about the senator. And I was up that way earlier on and the little bugger never reminded me.'

'I see, well, maybe you'd better get up there and do it straight away now, hadn't you?'

'Right, Canon, right, I'll straighten out the senator at once. Oh and by the way Canon, I wonder, with all this heat and everything, and with old Widow Claine after dyin' on us, if you'd be kind enough to get young Sean O'Boyle up the day after tomorrow to help me fill in poor Sally's grave. I'm a bit weak in the legs these days, it's the heat you know, only the heat.'

'Very well, Francis Patrick, and I think I'll have him burn that old pile of rubbish you've gathered at the far side; and maybe you'd get the scythe at the rushes and thistles down at the other end?'

'I will, Canon, straight away at it now I'll be, mark my words, Canon, mark my words.'

Frankie stood up as the Canon turned back towards the sacristy. As soon as the door had closed Frankie sat down again.

At three o'clock the clutch of town notables, the pipe band in all their glory, kilts and feathers and buckled shoes, pipes and drums and the big bass drum, paraded past Frankie who was still sitting on the O'Rorke slab. They played their songs of lament by the senator's grave and they stood on the faces and chests and legs of all the lesser dead round about. The droning of the pipes and the heavy pounding of the drum drowned out all the stutterings of complaint. The notables flattened the grass behind the senator's grave and nobody, not even the Canon, noticed that the grass had not been trimmed. A stiletto heel stabbed into the ribs of an old labourer but the rattle of his bones was lost under the skittering of the snare drums. The Canon led a decade of the rosary. And blessed eyes were gazing up freely at lovely sights strictly denied them when they were alive and now no longer of any interest to them. After the playing of the National Anthem the pipers struck up O'Donnell Abú and everybody left the senator to his afternoon nap.

Frankie spent the afternoon with Sally O'Malley. They were both thirty years old, both plump and healthy and wildly happy in their love. It was body to body without drawback or shame or contrition, without lies or hesitations of double-talk, but strictly secret, for Sally's big-bodied generosity was also her source of income and Frankie, sacristan and grave-digger, wanted to hold down his job. That was the best year of Frankie's life and Sally told him it was her happiest too, her free giving allowing her to feel that her endowed body was more than just a duty imposed upon her, more than a means of livelihood.

But of course the Canon heard about it; he was then a mustard -hot raving recruit just out of Maynooth and he banished Frankie forever from his job as sacristan, telling him he was fit only to work among the dead; he denounced Sally by name from his Sunday pulpit and made every effort to have her driven from the island. But Sally was pregnant, and the people, in spite of a generally audible murmuring against her, knew her worth and did not move to ostracise her. Sheila was born and Sally never brought the child through the chapel door.

When Sheila, at the age of eight, died under the wheels of a truck, Canon MacHugh could not forbid her burial in sanctified ground and Sally, poor, poor sufferer, was too distraught to care. Sheila was buried in a barely-marked grave and Sally, loving Sally, never visited the grave, for she had no faith in sentimental drivelling and thought it better to campaign for a bypass to take the heavy trucks out of the village and send them harmlessly on their way. Sally, poor, true Sally, gone now, and the island left to all the windbags.

Francis Patrick Hanrahan, dressed in his finest suit, his waistcoat and tie, his silver cuff-links and his Sunday hat, attended the Mass for Sally O'Malley. Only the sacristan, the altarboy and an old woman from the mountain, were present. The Canon, no doubt, took pleasure in his choice of readings and went through the Mass with vindictive emphases. Only the altarboy received Communion, the old woman from the mountain not quick enough off her mark. The undertakers carried the coffin out the side door of the chapel and over the few yards of ground to the grave. They laid it on the wooden struts and placed the ropes under and around it, then stood back to wait. The Canon scattered a little water on the coffin, said a few loud Latin words and gave the signal. Sally was lowered into the grave, the struts removed, the Canon sprinkled in more water and a handful of pebbly words; Frankie drew across the artificial grass and that was that.

Late in the evening, Frankie returned, without his bicycle, but carrying his bag. He was still wearing his best suit, hat, waistcoat and tie, even his fob watch with its silver chain. He sat down on the O'Rorke slab and waited. When it was almost dark he took Sheila out from the bag and pushed the bag far in among the knotted boles of the yew trees. Then he pulled the grass blanket from Sally's grave, lowered the wooden ladder and climbed down.

'Never mind now, Sally love, never mind, you knew I wouldn't let you down.'

He unscrewed the coffin lid and lifted it off. Sally was not heavy, all the richness had been fretted away by the harshness of the world and by the integrity of her convictions. She was stiff, but Frankie managed to lift and push her up the ladder; she stood upright for one awful moment, fully out of the grave, before falling forward onto the mound of clay. Should the Canon have gazed out the presbytery window at that precise moment ...

Frankie climbed out after her, got her onto his wheelbarrow and set off across the graveyard to the northwest frontier. As carefully as he could he hoisted her up on the top of the great pyre and straightened her graveclothes about her. He had five gallon-drums of petrol hidden in the hedge and with these he doused her, and the branches, wreathes, plastics and withered stalks. Then he stood back, lit a match and flung it on the heap.

Soon the Canon, seeing the flickering light against his bedroom curtain, looked out and saw a fire raging at the end of the graveyard; he was pleased to see his gravedigger working on so late. When the fire had died down, some hour and a half later, Frankie took an eggcup from his jacket pocket, gingerly filled it with ash from the centre of the pyre and went back carefully to Sally's grave. He felt tired now, awfully tired; his whole body seemed to be ablaze with pain, and he knew he did not have a great deal of time left before that fire caught his heart and burned him out. He drew up the ladder out of Sally's grave and hid that, too, in the tangle of the yew trees. Now he was ready. Standing over the grave he scattered Sally's ashes out over the hole. Little specks of ash moved freely off under the night breeze, but most of it floated dreaming down into the open coffin below.

'The best I could do, love, the best I could do.'

Then he put Sheila inside his jacket, buttoned it tightly and slithered and climbed down into the grave. He drew the grass blanket over the gap above; the light went out, and all the stars. He climbed into the coffin and, with some difficulty because of his long legs, got himself fitted in. He placed Sheila's skull down between his knees and pulled the coffin lid as carefully as he could over them both. Now he was in darkness, and in a darkness within darkness, and he could close his eyes and rest.

'Now lads and lassies,' he said to all the cheering, welcoming host, 'let's only hope that Sean O'Boyle will be in a great race to get his day's work done.'

BETWEEN ISLANDS

It was not yet dawn, but she was up and dressed. She had scarcely slept and certainly had had no need of the alarm clock set for five. She spilled the milk at breakfast and dropped an egg onto the scullery floor. Nora O'Flaherty's hair had grown white and wispy during the last months; lines that had been waiting somewhere inside had appeared on her forehead, round her lips, along her cheeks; under her eyes the flesh had folded and hardened until the top of her cheeks had become ridged, like lazybeds.

'Have you the tickets, Owen?'

'Yes, mother, I have everything; stop fussing and fidgeting; I'll be fine, don't worry.'

They stood at Scanlon's cross in near darkness, under a hedge of fuchsia that leaned out over the wall; the bus reached the crossroads at twenty minutes past six and was in Westport in time to catch the train for Dublin. Now there was nobody on the road; the rain had stopped though an occasional drop gathered on the tips of the fuchsia flowers, hung there interminably, then plopped onto the road. The restraining wall opposite was dulled and darkened with the damp and a poster advertising Friday's film was drooping upon itself, sodden and dead.

'Have you got the apple tart? and the soda bread?' she asked him, happier to think of these stout supplies in his bag during the journey, happier to break the silences that hung between them.

'Yes, yes, I have all of them, here, look, in this bag.'

Nora frotted her fingers along her coat, as if she was remembering the dough still sticking to them and falling off in little worm shapes of loss onto the floor. She remembered how the waters had broken, oh how many years ago! in those primrose days when all the world cohered! how he had put his head out through the fissure in her womb and screamed, how he always said he had a memory of it, as of standing in night-stillness at the edge of a huge expanse of water. There had been blood, of course, and she had known great pain. But then she had held him, moulding him like white dough in her hands. How he had enjoyed, later, the dried currants she had given him from the cake-making and how he would run from her out into the grove to eat them and then, while she stood rubbing her hands and leaning against the red door of the house, she would watch him swing on the lower branches of the trees; how green he was, then, but how his eyes were deepening, like darkening berries.

She was silent now, while they waited. She longed to reach out and hold him hard against her, as a drowning person would cling to a floating spar. But he was too old for that now, he was free of her, independent, an island awash on his own ocean. He was shifting gently from foot to foot as if he had already spent years aboard ship, as if the earth beneath his feet were rolling in its passage across the waters of space.

'You will write to me, Owen, won't you? As soon as you get a chance you will write?'

'Yes, mother, I promise, I will write. Whenever the ship touches port I'll write. And it won't be that long till I'm back home for a spell and then I'll be with you for about three months.'

Somewhere through the air there was a stirring; the day would darken and the storms would come; waves would rise over the harbour wall, tickling the curraghs lying face down under ropes and stones. That perpetual movement of the sea was in her blood, too, and she knew it, it had always been there, the restlessness that the ocean breeds, the need to hear its breathing, to feel its surge and fall in the beating of your heart.

The bus appeared on the top of the long slope leading down to Scanlon's cross; at first only its eyes were visible, those wide, dim lights that brought it through the dawning; then they could hear it, changing gears towards the bottom of the hill, gathering hold, preparing for the turns. Nora reached out suddenly and gripped him and a flood of anguish reached upwards from the depths of her soul. He yielded to her and sank his head once more on her bosom, knowing the warm smell of her, the hugeness of her simple love, the emptiness he was leaving to her after all. Then he was gone, the small red lights of the bus so quickly passing round the monastery turn, vanishing into the future and into the past.

As she turned back towards the silent house she found herself repeating the names of places on her island with sudden affection, Rusheen, Lake Nakeeroga, Bulls Mouth, Breann Ascaill, Bun an Churraigh, Dun Inbhir dá Tonn, familiar places she had often been to, with him; then she spread her arms out to the sky, like wings, and pleaded: now Lord, now, let my heaviness lift from the earth into your loving arms.

~

Nora follwed Owen's progress on an old school atlas; she would take the strange stamps off the envelopes and imagine his life from them. Papua New Guinea, stamps with the *sagra speciosa* and the *marpesia acilia tervisia*, strange coloured creatures suggesting light and sunshine and deep, tangled undergrowth. Tasman's Arch. Tete and Poaka birds of New Zealand. Siapo makers and naked chieftains of Samoa. Fiji, the Gilbert Islands, dugouts and flying foxes. The red Lauan trees and the Capu-Lapu of the Philippines.

Then the letters began to be less frequent, he seemed to take great leaps across the world, from Australia to China, from China to South Africa, and once, the closest yet, he wrote from some great port in Greece. He was happy, he always told her, working in the engine room of a trading ship, friendly with the crew, people from all over the world, from all continents, coloureds, whites, blacks ... The ship was large, and sound, all the typhoons and all the storms of the seven seas could scarcely touch her. He said. And went silent.

~

Dear Owen,

I am writing this in the kitchen. It is early, about eight o'clock, but I have been up for a long while. I have made soda bread and an apple tart but I don't know who's going to eat them. My fingers are sensitive still from the dough. The kitchen has been warmed with the smell of the baking. It is the smell that reminds me of you, it is your smell.

The days have grown very long for me now and I search about the house for chores; I find myself shifting vases from one place to another, as if it mattered. There cannot be many days left to me now. But enough of that. Perhaps if you were to come home now you'd find it dull.

I fret at any sound of the wind rising. Sometimes at night, when I pray beside the bed or when I sit just watching the fire, I can hear the sea about the island gather all its force to fling against the shore; the sound comes reaching down the chimney, and it rattles the frames of the windows and the doors. I cry then, sometimes, because I think of you and I know the seas where you are must be wild and strange. There have been so many losses. Enough of that. Forgive me. Please write.

Do you remember? I gave you coping saw and glue, breast drill

and plywood, you made a Viking ship, you carved stern and prow
like the ends of a pew in the Monastery Chapel; for mast and boom
you took my knitting needle and a piece from an apron that had tiny
red stars on it, and then you sailed the boat down the stream beyond
our gate; do you remember the day? you were six or seven and Oh
I was sorry then because the excitement in you was so great you
could not find the words. Please write. The sea is in our blood,
Owen, and it will not rest. Please write.

The kitchen is filling up with your smell. When you come home
perhaps you'll find it dull. I leave the yard light on through these,
the darkest nights.

~

Nora walked the island roads, an ordinary old woman filled
with sadness. She visited the graveyard where her husband,
Donal, sheathed in a brown habit, lay in the womb of earth,
slimed with the afterdeath; stone angels drowned under
foxglove, montbretia, grass; columbine was an ocean weed
draping her daughter's bed and over it lay a fishing-net and
four glass globes that had been used as marker buoys; and
there was her name, Patricia, drowned at the age of twenty-
one, lying now under the waves of the earth, listening out,
with her father, for the distinctive footsteps of the One who
had walked on water.

She wandered by the shore, watching where the Atlantic
narrowed between mainland and island, a deep wound
where the current rushed, now one way, now the other,
where the old O'Malley tower house stood, an empty shell
that once guarded the approaches to the island. Here lay
hidden the memory of Grace O'Malley, pirate queen, ances-
tor to Nora O'Malley, widow, and to her dead husband,
Donal. Nora went in to the damp hollow darkness of the
tower and watched out through one of the narrow slits over
the sea. The blood in her veins flowed, she thought, noisily,

like the wash of the current, the surge almost audible, tangible, a hurt.

Only the postman, Michael, noticed how thin and worn she had become. She was always looking out for him but when he called it was only for a chat; there were few letters now, few cards. One evening, when the winds were sounding in the chimney, the door opened and her husband, Donal, came in. He said nothing to her, hardly seemed to notice her, but she could see that he was soaked through to the flesh. She got up to make his supper while he sat warming himself by the fire. One of the things she loved most was to take a fresh mackerel and fry it for him in butter; she put on the pan, cut a great blob of butter and placed it pan to melt. When it was sizzling she went to the sink where the fish would be; but there were no fish, there was only the empty sink, the slow, eternal drip, drip, drip from a tap. When she came back to the fire he was gone. Only then the terror came upon her. That night she cried herself into an uneasy sleep.

She told Michael what had happened.

'You should eat a bit more, Nora,' he said; 'you're not looking after yourself, you'll have to keep your strength up. You never know when Owen will be back and he'll want to see you in good shape. Eat lots, Nora, eat lots.'

So she cooked Owen's favourite dish, potato cakes; she cooked a lot of them and placed a dish of hot cakes on the table, with butter melting over them and dribbling down onto the plate, and she sprinkled them with sprigs of freshly cut parsley. Owen came in from the yard and sat down to eat. She sat in her corner, content, watching him. He delighted in the cakes and when he had finished she shifted the iron kettle onto the open fire and waited for it to boil. As she poured water into the teapot to scald it she turned towards him, but he had gone, leaving no sign. The cakes were untouched, a slight scum had begun to settle on the butter.

'I'll ask Doctor Weir to call on you, Nora,' Michael promised;

'it's just a slight turn you had, that's all. A good tonic will soon put the blood back into your veins.'

~

Dear Mother,

I have at last found somewhere I will be able to call home. It's an island, Western Samoa, in a little village on the Pacific coast. It's beautiful. Some people even say that this is where Paradise used to be. We get hurricanes here; there are mangrove forests along the coast. They say Robert Louis Stevenson is buried here somewhere.

You would laugh if you saw our house. The floor is made of stone and there are mats of coconut leaves all over the floor. The roof is thatch, but it's a thatch made out of palm leaves. One wall of the house is also made of leaves so that on very hot days you'd laugh to see us rolling up the wall of the house to let in the light and air.

The strangest thing has happened. Over here, in Ipolu, one evening in a bar in Apia, I met a girl who was born in Aughagower, just outside Westport, and do you know what? her name is Ellen O'Malley! There! She came out here some years ago with lay missionaries, loved the place, and stayed. Mother, we are going to be married! She is my own age, and lovely. I am very, very happy. Next month we get married. We are going on our honeymoon to New Zealand. We'll be there about two weeks as my ship has to call in there. Then we'll come back to live here. Some time after we're really settled in, I'll come home and visit. I might even persuade Ellen to come along. I know you'll love her, and I know she'll love you, too.

~

Late that evening Doctor Weir, searching for Nora O'Malley O'Flaherty, found her sweeping the clay floor of the old tower house, trying to dust the high, stone walls, and to clear away the rubbish thrown down over the years by hordes of tourists come to sense the presence of the old pirate, to imagine the rush of her wild blood along their own dull veins.

THE SECRET LOVE-LIFE OF OLLIE GUNNING

Ollie Gunning stood gazing out his newly-finished attic window. It was a wet morning; swathes of mountain rain fell in across the suburbs, frustrating the women with their washing-machines, annoying the postman beyond words, creating a dark, miasmic rain-forest.

Ollie had floored part of the attic, using the best tongued-and-grooved timber he could find, slotting just enough planks together to make a platform leading from the trap-door across the naked beams to the window. The ceiling of his bedroom was not reinforced; that would have been too expensive and something he would not be able to do himself. The electric wiring criss-crossed the floor like dark lianas. He laughed to himself, rubbing his hands fretfully along the sides of his thighs; *putting your foot in it*, now wasn't that a fine expression? you could so easily put a foot wrong up here and come through, like the roots of a tree, into the bedroom below. The pity was that there was a drip coming in where he had not fixed one of the joints perfectly enough. A drip in an attic is not a great thing ... it can cause trouble, like an obsession in the brain ... still, the attic window would serve, that's what mattered.

He glanced casually out the window, a Tarzan surveying the jungle acres of suburbia, across his back garden, over his high walls, and was just able to see the bedroom window of number 18 Heatherfield Rise. For a moment his heart thumped crazily. The curtains had just been drawn back and he knew that Andrea was in that room; dressing? undressing? Perhaps, if he went back downstairs for the binoculars ... ? He cursed himself soundly for the thought. And anyway hadn't he locked away the binoculars in a cupboard in the spare room and locked the key of the cupboard in his wall safe in an effort to make it difficult for himself to take that course. In any case, it is impossible to see any distance into a room when there's no light inside.

Andrea, he thought, was up earlier than usual; perhaps her pilot husband had come home last night and was now demanding his breakfast? his ... *oats!* (the word roared like a chainsaw in Ollie's brain) ... or maybe he was coming home today and she had to get the place in shape? Ollie turned suddenly from his attic window and went downstairs to fry up some black pudding for his own breakfast. He had nobody to whom he was in servitude; he had no responsibilities; he was free, a prowling wildcat; a hawk resting on the topmost branches; wasn't he the wise man to stand clear of all duties and demands!

Ollie Gunning was forty-nine years old, frightened of the number fifty, still handsome, swarthy, well-built, balding. Since the workers at the Leviathan Hardware Store had been let go, Ollie knew he would never find employment again. While that fact did relieve him of the last vestiges of real responsibility in his life, he still bemoaned the fact that he would have to make all his own decisions, every moment of every day, for the rest of his life. He had time on his hands and time was a permanent itch somewhere just under the skin. He had the back garden of his house, number 26 Heatherfield Close, to develop.

Ollie had ordered three tons of top-soil and laid out a fine vegetable garden. Then he had built a greenhouse and bought in several well-developed peach trees and a vine. In his vegetable plot he worked on asparagus, iceberg lettuce and mange-tout. None of your cabbages and onions for Ollie Gunning! The greenhouse he had built tended to sag in the middle where the timber frame had to be lengthened with bits of wire but, on the whole, it would serve. He had brought around a small basketful of peaches, (ahhhh! peaches) to Andrea Spiers-Mitchell.

Brrrriiiiing! Brrrriiiiing! He waited, nervous, shuffling. His mind, and his body, were confused. Why was he doing this? He had dressed casually, but carefully. Had raked his few wisps of hair across the barren lawn of his skull. He had shaven. Tried out his new, Brut aftershave. His new Brut anti-perspirant deodorant. His new Brut splash-on lotion. Arranged the suburban peaches on a bed of straw in a small, wicker basket. He knew she was at home. Hadn't he been watching her, through his binoculars, from the upstairs window as she lay, half-naked, on the sunbed in her back garden, the strap of her bra undone (she must have dozed off, it must have slipped) so that the sun could caress her ... and he knew that pilot husband of hers was away... Burma or somewhere!

She opened the door. She was wearing a florid, exotic dressing-gown. She was a lavish jungle of birds-of-paradise, dense undergrowth, exuberant fruits. Ollie gasped. That peach flesh, those ice-cream teeth, those big, green eyes, those swelling breasts, those full, curved hips ...

'Oh, Ollie, it's you ... '

'Me, Andrea, Mrs ahh, yes, sorry to bother you and all but, these peaches, you know, for Mr Mitchell, or I mean for you, I grew them myself, in the greenhouse, you know, first of the bunch, you might say, loads of them really, (*a lie*) I'd be glad, you might, ah, sample a few of them, with himself, of course ... '

'Oh Ollie! how wonderful! your own peaches. They're gorgeous, and aren't you clever? Imagine! peaches in Heatherfield!'

She had laughed, beautifully, her hand rising to her bosom, the dressing-gown slipping open a little more, the cleavage, that dark, soft tunnel ...

'Come in, Ollie, please do, come on in. I've got some cream. Perhaps we could take the skin off those peaches, whip up some cream and have a feast? Just you and me. I've got some Glenmorangie, too, Urban brought it home last time, duty free you know, so, peaches, cream and single malt? How's that sound? Urban's away, won't be back for a few days. Bangkok.'

Bangkok indeed. Naked peaches. Undressed. Whipped. Oh how innocent and virginal poor Andrea is. And how criminal of him to try and take advantage ...

'Oh, no, no thanks very much. Can't stop. Must build my wall you know. Walls ice-cream, what? ha-ha-ha. No thanks, no. Peaches. For you. Hope you.... Fruits to the fruit, what? (*going a bit far, that, eh?*) I mean, please, I've got loads of them. In the greenhouse. Don't throw stones. Don't throw the stones back. You know? Stones ... peaches ... people in glasshouses? 'Bye.'

He dumped the basket in her hands and walked away as quickly as he could, hands in his pockets, whistling. Irresponsible. Primitive. Free as a wildcat. Still, the thought of her eating his naked peaches, putting them into her mouth, delicately, those white teeth on the soft, juicy flesh ... He went home and searched for a place in which to lock away his binoculars.

Now he stood over his stove, frying great discs of black pudding while the rain clattered against the patio door. Since he had built the walls, darkness had descended on his garden and his greenhouse; the vegetables stretched, wan and lank, towards the sky, the trees and the vine in the greenhouse wilted, shivered and grew sad.

Ollie repapered and repainted the entire house; he took out the old fireplaces and built new ones. Then he moved into the garage and began to convert it into a workshop, breaking out a door between the hallway and the garage. To keep himself busy. To keep his mind active.

When Andrea Spiers and her husband, Urban Mitchell, moved into the house to the back of his, Ollie was stunned to pain by the sight of the beautiful, delectable, sensual young woman. Almost at once she had taken to sunning herself on the dull lawn of her back garden. She was an orchid, big and lush and frightening, suddenly a-bloom in the drab desert of Heatherfield, infinitely desirable in her skimpy bikinis beyond the fence that separated the two gardens. Quickly Ollie had had to sue for mercy.

'I'm, ah, Ollie Gunning. Live there, just behind you. Behind you. I'm at your back, so to speak. I'm ah wondering if you wouldn't object if I put up a little wall along between the gardens, for shelter for the garden, you see? ah, shelter.'

'Come in, come in Mr Gunning. My name's Andrea, Andrea Spiers, and now I'm married to Urban Mitchell so they call me Andrea Spiers-Mitchell. Frightful, isn't it? (*White blouse, tight, blue-grey jeans, emphasising, outlining, hair undone, oh God*) No, of course not, we don't mind. Anyway we're just renting this house until Urban finds somewhere more lavish. Come on in. Neighbours ought to be neighbourly, don't you find?'

'No. I mean, no, thanks, I don't, can't come in right now. Must dash, must get back. Not a child in the house washed yet, in a manner of speaking.'

'You have children, Mr Gunning? em, Ollie? if I may.'

Ollie. In her mouth. *Oll-lie* ... Sounded, suddenly like the name of a film star, a mega-lover, a Burt What's-his-name, Clint Who's-it, even a Michael George, or a George Michael, whatever.

'No, no, not married, no children, no, escaped all of that, never put to sea there, if you follow me, no ...'

And he had gone home to order his first load of bricks,

sand and cement.

Within three days Ollie Gunning had constructed a reasonably straight wall, seven feet high, between his back garden and the back garden of number 18 Heatherfield Rise. Now he could no longer see the rich valley opening down Andrea's lovely back as she lay on her sunbed in the garden. Slightly disconcerted for a while, Ollie decided he would build a boat in his half-converted garage. He bought the do-it-yourself kit, all the tools he needed, and it kept him occupied for a while. But one afternoon, as he was getting into overalls in his upstairs bedroom, he glanced out and saw Andrea working in her garden. She wore a dark red blouse that was tied up under her breasts, exposing her tanned midriff. As she stooped, in her short tennis skirt, Ollie's eyes rested for a while on the pink frills of her panties. Once again his heart and mind exploded in a transport of need and hurt and longing. He ran downstairs and ordered another load of bricks, cement and sand. He added another seven feet of wall onto the seven he had already constructed. When that was finished, he could no longer see into that garden from upstairs, he could barely see the top quarter of the bedroom window of her house. After all, if your right eye is scandalising you ...

Then Andrea called on Ollie, putting her lovely head round the garage door, to ask him if he wouldn't mind looking after her house while she was away for a few days — she was going to a bridge weekend with some *women* friends — Urban was in Boston and would be staying over there for the next few days, would Ollie come round and she'd explain the alarm system to him, give him the combination numbers, please, if he'd be so kind ...?

And so Ollie Gunning found himself standing up against her in the tiny cloakroom of number 18 Heatherfield Rise while she showed him the alarm keys and outlined the system to him. Then she led him upstairs to show him where the main board was, in the hot press, and to write out for him the combination of numbers, just in case ... She went upstairs ahead of him, lifting her immaculate tennis skirt as she rose, moving her body voluptuously, turning to smile at him. Ollie could see the shapely thighs swell into the unbearable fullness of her buttocks, he could glimpse the pink, demanding panties, that trellissed gateway to the garden of Eden. At the top of the stairs the bedroom door stood open, the pink duvet on the bed was smooth and welcoming, like a cool ocean after a long and searing desert crossing ... Ollie, trying to memorise the numbers for the combination, suddenly recalled that he was supposed to phone his dentist in five minutes time and he rushed away from her, down the stairs, and home.

He missed her then, missed the knowledge of her presence beyond his high walls, and when the weekend was over he took a chisel and bored a small hole in the cement between two of the bricks in the wall at the end of the garden. Putting his eye to the aperture he could see Andrea's garden once again. He saw her emerge from the back door, carrying her washing in a little plastic basin, and she began to hang up her private things on the line, close to where poor Ollie's eye was fastened. He went indoors and ordered another load of bricks, cement and sand and within three days had built a second wall, six inches inside the first wall, the bricks placed in such a way that if he were to bore a hole it would open out only onto brick.

That night, he lay in bed, sobbing and tossing in wakefulness. Then he lay still for a while, standing Andrea before his mind, murmuring her name to the darkness of his room, willing her to sense his calling, hoping that telepathy was a reality in life, calling her to him, urging her to come and take upon herself the responsibility of initiating action. The silence in his bedroom deepened, in spite of the perpetual distant susurration of traffic and the occasional echoing bark of a suburban dog coping with frustration somewhere in the suburban undergrowth. It was then Ollie knew he would have to build a window in the attic, to allow himself the opportunity of seeing Andrea once again ...

~

Andrea Spiers-Mitchell drew back the curtains of her bedroom window and looked out on a wet and windy morning. She was naked after a hot and heartening shower. She stood back suddenly as she had glimpsed Ollie Gunning's head at his newly-built window high in the roof. She sat on the edge of her bed for a while, gazing abstractedly across the spaces towards that window. Like looking through tree-tops, of steel and wood and slate. She found Ollie Gunning a mystery, handsome, yes, even exciting in a wild-tomcat sort of way, perhaps because of his obvious loneliness, perhaps because of his seeming indifference to everything she had done to inveigle him into action. Now she closed her eyes, tightly, and, still sitting naked and tingling on her bed, murmured his name out loud into the silence of the room, willing him to sense her calling, hoping that telepathy was a reality in life, calling him to her, urging him to come and take upon himself the responsibility of initiating action. Then she laughed at herself; perhaps she should have been more direct ... he did seem so innocent, so unaware, so carefree, so ... so virginal ... She stood up again and moved closer to the window, combing out her hair, stretching to the right, to the left, glancing towards that attic window. There was no sign of Ollie. And anyway, it was too late now.

Her suitcases were packed and waiting in the hall downstairs. So many wasted years gathered up and folded neatly into three suitcases! Urban, suave, glib, articulate, superficial Urban, high-flyer, low-liver, such a slug, such a wire-worm, such a snake! A slug in the cabbage of bliss. A snake in the forests of Eden. She knew there was a woman in Bangkok, and one in Boston, and no doubt there were others in Rome, Khartoum, Karachi ... wherever. And she, Andrea Spiers, recently young and hopeful, had become just the woman in Heatherfield. Urban, she could picture him, possibly at that very moment, in his captain's uniform, that extra-virgin-olive-oil voice of his when he spoke to his passengers, his lethal combination of Old Spice aftershave and Brut splash-on-all-over as he laid down his Gucci overnight bag, his casual handing over of a bottle of single malt — oh Christ! — and his laying out of a whole carpetful of lies and fraud and deceit to charm his women here and there and everywhere. Ugh! She had had enough of it. Fresh woods, now, and suburbs new.

For weeks the only excitement in her life had been Ollie Gunning, that little curling thrill she got when she thought how she might prove unfaithful to Urban and brighten up Ollie's drab life, and her own. That day he had introduced himself, she found him so utterly appealing, offering her his peaches! She was naked under her old dressing-gown, she liked being naked around the house, straddling the kitchen stools, lolling on the sofa, sipping a single malt at four o'clock, she knew her body was good, a gift from God, she felt best when naked or nearly naked. Fruits to the fruit indeed. And then she had got a whiff of his aftershave. Brut! oh God! And the thought of Urban had come upon her so overwhelmingly that she found herself quite dizzy. Later she had tried a peach; it was hard and bitter and would never ripen. She dumped them.

Andrea was glad when Ollie built his wall. It seemed to concentrate more warmth into her back garden. She began to spend more pleasant hours soaking in the gentle caressing sun of Heatherfield. When the phone rang one afternoon and she ran in to answer it, Urban's voice, smooth and distant, telling her he had to take an additional flight from Nairobi to Rio and would not be home for the weekend, gave her such a sense of relief that she had laughed aloud in her kitchen. As she lay on her back on the sunbed and loosened her bra as fully as she dared, her unvoiced prayer was for a hijacking of that flight and the very gentle, but firm, doing-to-death of the pilot. The insurance! the independence! ... and there was Ollie, suddenly, in his bedroom upstairs, binoculars to his eyes. Poor Ollie, birdwatching, no doubt, although only sparrows seemed to stir in the suburban rainforests of Heatherfield. She allowed her bra to slip gently off her breasts. She stretched herself luxuriously. The sun touched her, delicately.

~

When Mr and Mrs Spiers-Mitchell moved away from Heatherfield, Ollie Gunning was shattered. He spent some days in misery and gave up working on his boat to mope about the sad darkness and the glum aridity of his enclosed back garden. But soon he began to know relief. He ordered a skip, bought a wheelbarrow, a sledgehammer, a pickaxe and began to demolish the two high walls at the end of his garden. He spent several happy days trundling between garden and front gate, barrowing the rubble out into a series of skips that gladdened the heart of some builder in a distant suburb of the city. Ollie tidied up his garden, erected a delicate, white-mesh plastic fence at the end of the garden along which he would trail sweet-pea, and set to repairing the derelict green-house. He found himself whistling again, moving about his house with ease and pleasure. He began to think of finishing the boat and of getting a towbar fixed to his old car.

As Ollie Gunning was soaking in his bath at the end of a busy day, he was not aware that Kevin Johnston and Betsy-Ann, his young bride, had just moved in to 18 Heatherfield Rise. Betsy-Ann was red-haired, plump and attractive, anxious to please, gregarious and bright-eyed. Kevin

Johnston was an engineer who worked with an oil company. He would have to spend three weeks away on an oil-rig in the North Sea, then come home for three weeks, then go away for two months ... leaving Betsy-Ann to fend for herself among the high walls and enticing cul-de-sacs of Heatherfield Heights.

THE WORD 'STONE'

John Twin Fadian watched his head mirrored in the clear water of a rock pool. He opened his mouth and saw the word come out like a stone and plop into the water. 'Cloouuurck!' was the sound he made. It was like the beginning of a cough, or a vocalised gulp, John Twin's tongue being too big for his mouth, the sounds getting stuck somewhere between his chest and the roots of his tongue. Tony, twin brother, could speak perfectly; but then Tony was ordinary in every way, normal, un-crooked, having come out first, John reluctantly following.

By late morning the ocean would have come in again and covered this pool, disturbing the life established there, adding new life and the nourishment of algae. It was marvellous. John Twin could sound so many of the words in his mind, so many things that were swimming around or floating or just holding on in the miniature ocean of the pool, or in the wider world of the Atlantic, words like anemone, periwinkle, barnacle, crab, sea slug, dead-men's-fingers, kelp; delicious sea-words that made him salivate between the teeth, filling his mouth with their salt taste, sparkling like sunlight on the ocean of his brain.

He watched a tiny, light-green crab sidle out from under a stone and move as if it had a purpose, crossing the floor with the delicacy of a slow foxtrot and disappearing under another stone on the opposite side. He wondered what assignation was involved, what little bit of labouring, of building, or, perhaps, of loving ... He watched the blob of an anemone, its dark plum-coloured shape, minuscule tentacles plucking algae from the water. It was important to be able to put words on things, John Twin knew, to be able to pick out nourishment from the awful mess that is the universe and name it in its accessible parts, divide it into manageable proportions of actual truth, take it into his soul and refer to it, even if only in the echo-chamber deep within himself.

He put his hand into the water, watched it change shape under the surface, become distorted; he laughed out loud at the funny twist of it; 'arm', he sounded the word deep in his mind, 'arm, hand, fingers,' but they did not really look like his arm and hand and fingers, not there, shimmering, corkscrewed by the water. Sometimes the words did not quite tally with the objects, then that could be funny — or it could be a lie. He reached for a stone he could see on the bottom of the pool; the floor was further than he had thought and the rolled-up sleeve of his shirt became wet as he reached. He grasped the stone and drew it out; it was beautiful, 'stone', hard and true, smoothed by waves, fretted until it had become this shape — like a large egg.

John Twin laughed again; perhaps, he thought, if I sit on it long enough it will hatch out into a whole lot of little stones. He put it into the pocket of his waistcoat, picked up his bucket and began to clamber over the rocks of the shore towards the sea's edge.

Above his head a black-backed gull swooped towards him, letting out a screech of anger or surprise.

'Cloouuuurck!' it screamed at him.

'Clooooouuuurck!' John shouted back at the bird and he shook his fist into the air. The gull flew away, out over the waves, clean and big and lovely.

How good to be alive on such a sun-filled morning, the world alert all about him, the sun sparkling on rock and wrack, on cliff and field, over rock pool and ocean, each sparkle was different and each sparkle lovely in its own way. He was looking for barnacles and edible periwinkles, perhaps some moss for the making of puddings. Since his father had left for Coventry in search of work over three years ago and had never returned, the Fadian family were poor indeed. He imagined the dinner they could have, purely from the generosity of the sea: a soup from the remains of yesterday's pollock, a meal of barnacles and periwinkles boiled in milk, a dessert of carrageen moss to delight their bodies and enliven their souls. It would form his contribution today to the family income.

'Bar - na - cle; per - i - win - kle; moss;' what a lovely feel that last word had as it dropped its stringy softness into the pool of his brain. He could see the pale yellow flesh of the barnacle curl up in the boiling milk, come loose from its shell and offer its wholesomeness to the spoon. 'Barnacle, spoon, spoonbarnacle;' a right relationship of sounds, hardness of shell, softness of the l's of the flesh, finality of the word 'spoon'. Spoooooo - oooooonnn. And barnacle slips down the throat as easily as water. Periwinkle, a thin word, a long word, like the soft tail of the flesh that would uncoil from the shell as a pin dipped in and coaxed it out; smoothly, gently, the whispering unwhorling of the long word, the caution and precision of the pin.

John filled the can, listening always to the infinitely slow movement of the barnacle shells against the aluminium walls; a sad sound, a knocking, a pleading ... but they were innocent creatures, they knew nothing of death, they knew nothing of the harsh struggle that a poor family has to make to survive in this land, they didn't even know the word 'barnacle', they knew nothing; perhaps, John thought for a moment, perhaps they were the lucky ones ...

He turned for home. He left the shore and climbed into Harte's field. He followed a roughly-walled path round the edge of the field, naming buttercup and cowslip and daisy, wondering about the name 'cowslip'; does a cow really ...? or perhaps it was cow's lip, the little flower just reaching high enough to be ripped out by the moist hardness of the cow's lip? He must watch them the next time he saw Harte's cows in the field. Over the ditch, onto the rough road leading up to the main road. It was Sunday; people would be at Mass, muttering words they hardly understood, words they had mouthed so often they were now empty shells, their juices evaporated.

He came as far as the yard of the Church at the edge of the village. The people were inside; there were some who had taken up their stations leaning against the wall on either side of the great, wooden door outside. They would stay there until the last words were said and then they would go home, or to the pub. John Twin liked to join them, to lean against the wall alongside them; they laughed often, softly, they said funny things, they cracked jokes and he could laugh as heartily as any of them. Sometimes, too, they joked at him, but he didn't mind; they knew his angers, knew, too, that he was strong enough to make them know his feelings if he needed to, even if he couldn't say it to them in words. He heard the voice of the Canon inside, 'Twenty-first Sunday in ordinary time ... In the beginning ...'

The murmuring of the men, the warmth of the sunshine, the exertions of the shore, made John drowsy. He leaned back against the wall and dozed. But then he came to with a start, the men around him buzzing with excitement. A black Mercedes had drawn up outside the low periphery wall of the Church yard, and several men had got out. They were well dressed, wore suits and had hats. One of them held a number of printed sheets. Then another was helped up onto the wall while loudspeaking equipment, speakers, a microphone, were being set up. John Twin loved the sound of the static, the 'testing, testing, onetwothreefour, onetwothreefour' that was spoken before everything was ready. It was the Fianna

Fáil politician for this part of the county, Edward J. Finn, there was going to be some sort of election coming soon.

When the people came out from Mass they formed little groups in the yard of the Church. Now there was music playing through the loudspeaker; it seemed to build everyone into some sort of expectancy. The music stopped; one of the men stood up beside Finn and began to shout into the microphone.

'Ladies and gentlemen, may I have your attention please! It gives me great pleasure to introduce ...'

John Twin Fadian looked into his can; the mass of black and brown shells was still heaving slowly; he should have put some seawater in along with them; they would be suffering in the sunshine. He could see the feelers searching, the eyes out on sockets, he could sense their wonderment, the dismay of the poor creatures. Soon he would have to get home, soon, but first he would share some of the excitement in the Church grounds.

Finn was standing at the microphone. He raised his right hand into the air in a gesture of triumph, then his left, then he lifted both hands together and shook them tightly over his head as if he had just won some boxing contest. He drew a half-hearted ripple of applause out of the waiting people.

'My dear friends, my fellow Mayomen, my fellow Irishmen! I am deeply honoured to be here amongst you this lovely morning, and to share in your prayers and to stand in the grounds of your lovely Church. It is always a pleasure to be with you on this your lovely island, a place of true beauty, famous throughout Ireland, and indeed famous much farther afield, in every country around the world.'

John Twin thought of his father in England; perhaps he was not in England any more, perhaps he had moved on to Cleveland, in America, where a lot of his friends would be. Someone standing near to John muttered 'the oul' cod! he hasn't been on the island since the last election.'

'You know, my dear friends, that there is an election coming a month from now and I am here this morning to ask you to support my party in that election. I have been your representative in Dáil Éireann now for several years and you have seen your prosperity grow during those years, you have seen the tourists come in their thousands, nay, I would suggest, in their hundreds of thousands, to enjoy your hospitality and to give you of their bounty. You have seen the wealth of this nation grow along with the wealth of your lovely island.'

Somewhere there was a loud guffaw among the listeners. John Twin looked to see who had laughed. His brother Tony stood in a group of men nearby. John grinned over at him. 'Clourck!' he whispered.

'I am here to ask you to give your vote, your number one vote to Sean Frayne in the coming election and I can promise you that he will help you, he will help me, he will help us all, towards that great future you see before you.'

Once again Finn raised his fist over his head and punched the air in emphasis. There was a little applause, some shuffling. An old man standing near John muttered, not loudly enough to be heard, 'and what about the fishermen, why are they being forced to stop their fishing? why don't you stop the Spanish from trawling the fish out of our seas?' John nodded his head vigorously; he elbowed the man beside him and nodded towards the politician, but the old man only winked at him.

'We are doing everything possible to make this lovely country even more prosperous. You have seen our country take its place among the nations of Europe.'

His fist pounded at the sky.

'In this country the family has always been number one. And we in Fianna Fáil have a proud record of fighting for the sanctity of the Irish family.'

Someone shouted from the back of the crowd: 'And what

about emigration?' John Twin grunted his approval of the question.

'I say the family, the Irish family, we shall tend its sanctity, its primacy, against the forces that would destroy it. And Sean Frayne will continue this great crusade, together we will stand firm against every attempt to subvert the Irish family. This I stand for, this I insist upon, for this I will go on fighting!'

Finn's voice had risen high; the well-dressed men standing beside him cheered and applauded; John Twin grunted. One of the periwinkles in his can had worked its way up the side and was about to climb over the rim; John twitched it back down again. He was wondering where the prosperity was. Someone else shouted from the crowd: 'Why don't you bring our people home?' The shout was answered by a long chorus of approval. John spoke his word, quietly, 'Clouuuurck!'

'We are doing everything possible to bring our emigrants home. They are exiles from this fair land and we are going to set up an agency to look into their problems. We are creating employment at home and it will not be long before the people, our people my dear friends, come to know that their place is here, at home, with their families.'

John thought of his mother and her misery, of their home, its poverty, its limited and limiting wholesomeness, of their few unploughable, sodden fields, of the dinner he would make for them all. Why should his father come home to that ... why wouldn't they give his mother the money she needed ... she fought for it, but she got nothing ... he was not telling the truth, up there on the wall.

The other men were moving among the people, handing out leaflets. One of them passed near John, reached a leaflet towards him, then smiled and drew it back, offering it instead to the old man at John's side. John snarled and grabbed the leaflet. He gazed at what he had in his hand: a picture of E.J. Finn, smiling, well-fed, smug, and underneath it a photograph of Sean Frayne and a vote-number-one demand. John looked up at the man on the wall. In his brain something had begun to seethe; it was like the tide coming to stir up the crevices in the rocks; there was a sense of anger, he wanted to name that anger, he tried to shout but all that came from his mouth was a low growl; the frustrations of his life seemed to burst on him like spray from a wave. He trembled, he tried again to shout his anger but the man was loud now, confusing, he was surrounded by a haze of scarlet light, his body seemed to have grown enormous on the wall, to be swollen like a thundercloud, to be darkening the sky. John could not even get his inarticulate sound to come out.

Then the can fell from his grasp and the living mollusks spilled out between the feet of the people. Several were squashed at once and John dropped to his knees to save what he could of his work. The tears were blinding him, people jostled him, walking on the shells that exploded with little crackling sounds. The stone he had picked up from the rock pool fell onto the ground before him.

John Twin Fadian grew still and calm. He picked up the stone and stood erect. He could feel the smoothness and the weight of the stone, he thought of it again as an egg containing within it a myriad of tiny stones. It would burst, it would hatch beautifully against the head of the liar. He heard the sound deep within his brain, 'stone', strong, immediate, truth. He drew back his arm and flung it with all his strength and saw it fly straight and true towards its mark.

AN INSTRUMENT OF PEACE

The kesh had been unused for years; planks were broken, there were gaps and blacknesses, as in the mouth of an old man; supporting stakes had been eaten by the water and several looked as if they could collapse at any moment. The Gillespies had taken to dragging their boat up on the sandy shore of the lake, tying a rope from it round a large boulder near a fence and cursing the Irish weather. The giant otter had appeared close to the end of the kesh that reached out into the lake; he was oily, they said, and ugly, the size of a legless horse and he rolled under and over the surface of the lake, displaying terrible teeth and malign, enormous eyes. He could surface anywhere without warning and disappear again without leaving a ripple; he was a terror, a scourge for which there was no cure.

Richard and Helen and Mary Rose, although they had never seen the otter, did not dare stray onto the kesh; and of course they dared not swim, even though the summer days were hot and slow and long and even though, sometimes, the brown waters of the lake idled in golden patterns at the edge of the sand and butterflies and dragonflies swooped low across the surface. Anyway, the shallow, sandy beach ended suddenly in a cliff; you could drop over that cliff and down through the black water, down and down and down, to be sucked — if the otter didn't get you — into the foul ooze of the lake bottom.

Helen turned ten at the beginning of summer. Sometimes

she wondered how the monster never seemed to bother her father or Old Tom when they went out fishing, nor the German tourists who spent days on the lake in Andy Gillespie's small, fibre-glass boat. Once, when Helen had taken off her shoes and stockings and had paddled out until the water came high over her knees, all that had happened was that a horrible, black worm had slithered across her foot, bubbles had risen from between her toes and had tickled her gently as they rose along her legs and Old Tom had shouted at her to get the fucking hell out of the water. Then he had gone and told her parents; her father had slapped her hard across the backs of the legs and had told her she could be sure that the Christmas Angel would not come this year to such a bold, such an unbiddable child.

The great difficulty was that Aunt Deirdre had come with a gift for Richard — a model cabin-cruiser, painted green and yellow, with a tiny Irish flag on the stern, a real engine hidden inside and a wire rising out of it like a TV aerial; it worked by radio, by turning the knob on a handset that came with the boat. The Gillespies lived about a hundred yards from the lake but they could only try the boat on a shallow, stony stream that ran down beside the bushes of the back yard, through the kitchen garden, under the fence and out into the lake beside the kesh.

One day Richard had the handset and he should have pressed 'reverse' when the boat began to shoot the rapids and hit the narrower and deeper race of water going in under the fence. He let the handset fall and ran to watch the boat as it went, engine humming, out into the lake. Mary Rose screamed with anger but Helen was already over the fence and heading for the lake. She ran, tucking up her dress tightly into her pink knickers onto which there was a little yellow lily embroidered. When she got to the sand she flung off her shoes and stockings and was in the water before Mary Rose and Richard had got over the fence. The boat, still purring sweetly, became lodged in a gap in one of the rotted supports of the kesh and was waiting for rescue.

'No, no, Helen, you'll be destroyed! The cliff is just there and even the otter might be in that close.' Richard's voice began as an authoritative shout and then faded down the register into silence.

Mary Rose stood, her thumb in her mouth, her right hand pinching her chubby tummy. Helen was wading out, the water reaching over her knees, then touching the edge of her knickers. It was no good. She could not reach. She came back to the shore, perplexed.

'OK,' she said, 'I'll have to go out on the kesh.'

Richard burst: 'You can't do that! It's not allowed. Daddy'll kill you, he'll kill you, he'll kill us all!'

But Helen was moving out, cautiously, stepping on the more solid beams along the side of the kesh.

'It's grand,' she called back, 'it's not dangerous at all.'

She knelt down and leaned out over the post but the green and yellow boat was too far below her fingers.

'The oar!' she shouted, 'get the oar!'

Mary Rose went to the boat and lifted out an oar at least three times her own height. She came a little way onto the kesh, then reached and pushed the oar towards Helen. Helen shoved it down into the water and the blade slipped in under the kesh and caught on something there. She tugged hard; slowly the oar came up and with it a small network of yachting rope, orange-coloured and blue, and attached to it a white plastic drum just visible under the surface of the lake. Helen was frightened as the shape loomed under the water.

'It's a dead person!' she shouted.

'No, it's not,' said Mary Rose, who was at the edge of the kesh; 'it's only a barrel, or something.'

At last the blade of the oar came free and the barrel shape sank slowly back into its darkness. Helen got the end of the oar against the boat and gave it a shove. It came loose and moved out again into the lake, heading away from the shore.

'Oh no!' Helen shouted. Mary Rose began to cry.

'Turn it off! turn it off!' Helen called and Richard ran back to the fence, clambered over and got the handset; he pressed the button and the engine died. But the boat was floating away, still under the impetus of its engine, out towards the furthest edge of the kesh. Only then did they see the woman.

She was sitting on the extreme end of the kesh, where it was impossible to be, her legs dangling over the lake where the otter only had to surface, open his mouth and suck her in. She had a long, thin, fishing rod which she prodded into the boat's cabin and lifted it clean out of the water like a fish.

'Gotcha!' she laughed and stood up, walking easily back along the kesh towards the children. She was beautiful, tall and young, her skin dark as if she had been out all summer under the sun, but it was her hair! black and shiny so that the blue of the sky was in it, and the sunshine gold of the lake was there too, and the darkest and most starfilled night sky, and it went falling over her shoulders down to her waist; she had to move her head often, to swing it back from before her face. Her eyes were big and brown, filled with light and kindness and a glimmer of wickedness.

'I'll bet she'll tell on us,' Richard said later.

'She won't tell,' said Helen, 'I know she won't, she said so, and anyway wasn't she out there herself on the kesh and she'd only get into trouble too.'

The children were down at the lake again the following morning, early, and she was there, with a fire of twigs and driftwood crackling in a little circle of stones; her hair was wet, she had it tied up in a ball on the back of her head; she wore a pink blouse, and grey stone-washed jeans. She was cooking a fish that she had hung across the blaze on a piece of wire.

'Are you a traveller?' Mary Rose asked her at once.

'Yes, I suppose I am, in a way,' the woman answered.

'Would you like some fish?'

'I hate fish,' said Richard. So Mary Rose hated fish, too. Helen wasn't too keen but the smell was good and she said she'd try a bit. The woman took the fish from the fire and put it on a tin plate; she broke off some of the white flesh with her fingers and handed it to Helen.

'Mmmmm, it's just delicious,' said Helen.

The woman laughed and wolfed into the fish as if she hadn't eaten for days.

'You should use a knife and fork,' Mary Rose scolded.

'Were you out swimming?' Richard asked her.

'Yes; in the mornings the water is clear and cool. I had a lovely swim, and now I'm having my breakfast.'

There was no sign of a towel, or a tent, or even a bicycle, anywhere along the shore; there were no bathing togs hanging on bushes to dry.

'Did you swim with nothing on?' Mary Rose asked.

'Yes, I did, it was lovely. By the way my name is Clare. How are you, Mary Rose, Richard, Helen?'

She shook hands with them and they were only half surprised that she knew their names.

'The giant otter will get you,' Mary Rose warned.

'Oh I don't think so,' Clare answered, 'I don't think the giant otter will bother me. Aren't you lucky to have such a lovely lake right behind your house. Well,' and she licked her lips clean, 'I've got to go now. Maybe I'll see you here again?'

Clare came every morning then but by the time the children were up and ready she had been out for her swim and was waiting for them, cooking her breakfast, or just standing in the water, gazing out over the lake, her shoes held lightly in one hand. She chatted with them; sometimes they ate a little with her, even Richard tempted at last and relishing the taste. No, she was not married, she told them, although she would have liked to be, if circumstances had been different. But she was very happy, and no, she did not live in a house and no, she was not from around here. But wasn't it such a beautiful spot, so peaceful, so lovely, nature is so beautiful, isn't it?

The hot July days were drawing to a close. Soon it would be August; already, around the lake, trees were hanging more heavily, waiting for the depradations of the fall. The fields were sore under their cocks of hay; in some fields there were giant turds of hay gathered into black plastic bags, festering in their own heat. A yellow lethargy settled on the countryside. In the town the days of the Portiuncula were upon them and Richard, Helen and Mary Rose, with their parents, prepared to spend a day 'doing the visits'.

In the morning everyone dressed in Sunday clothes and they set off, very early, the car alert with a festive spirit. They were in the town by ten thirty and drove straight to the Church. But there were scarcely half a dozen cars in the grounds when they arrived and only three stalls selling religious objects.

The Gillespies felt their anticipation die to disappointment, the family, self-conscious now in their best clothes, and knowing themselves strangers in the small town, crossed the road and entered the Church. They knelt at the back for a few minutes; Richard sneezed, of course, and the children snickered; their mother hushed them, a harsh look quickly sharpening her weary face. Then they got up, having put themselves into the Presence, and left the Church.

They went into the chapel across the yard; it was small, rich with the scent of polish and incense, old and wise with the chants and visions of centuries, an apse of the chapel belonging to the Convent; here they knelt, sideways to the altar, with a high barrier of gilt bars and strengthened glass separating them from the cloistered saints. Helen strained to catch a glimpse of one of the sisters within, those who lived for ever behind high grey walls, who ate self-chastisement and drank the vinegar of prayer, who spent day and night in meditation before the Sacrament of Peace. Not even an edge of gimp or wimple could be seen from this angle.

They said the prescribed prayers. There were few worshippers in the chapel, three old women, a younger one, very fat, whose rosary beads made a rattling sound against the bench, and one old man whose prayers came out through his mouth as bees come out of a hive. Then the family stood up and went out the side door into the convent yard, along below a high wall and through a side-gate that brought them back into the Church yard, face to face again with the small chapel door. At this stage each member of the family had earned a plenary indulgence applicable to the souls in Purgatory; the children loved to imagine a soul released from the pains of punishment into the warmth of Heaven, soaring up from the ground into the brightest of skies and disappearing, murmuring its gratitude, waiting to help the children, in their turn, into Heaven.

They went back into the convent chapel and started all over again. Richard and Mary Rose, even Helen, were already bored. Their parents were less enthusiastic, missing the fervour and crush of the believers who had done the Portiuncula in years gone by. The third time they came into the chapel the children were ready to cry. And then, there she was, unmistakable, those jeans, that pink blouse, that midnight hair. She was in the front pew, her head in her hands, praying. Now the sun was brightening the chapel, the brass candle-sticks on the altar were dazzling in their sheen, the monstrance, with its golden spikes lovely as the brightness of a Van Gogh sun, shimmered and danced on the lovely lawn of the altar cloth.

The Gillespies finished their prayers and headed out the side door once more; Clare went out ahead of them. Mary Rose whispered, as loudly as she dared: 'Clare! Clare!' before they were quite out of the chapel, and her mother had to pinch her nastily on the behind. Clare did not turn round.

The Gillespie parents passed her by without noticing her, and then she turned and smiled back at the children.

'What are you doing here, Clare?' Helen asked.

'Amn't I doing the Portiuncula, like yourselves. This place is full of peace and love and service. But they never mention Francis and they should you know; after all, it's really Francis who began all of this ...' and she showed them a tiny leaflet with a funnily-shaped cross on one side and on the other the words of a prayer they had heard before: Lord, make me an instrument of your peace.

'I'd better be going,' Clare said. 'But I'll see you again, very soon.' And she walked away quickly towards the gate, waving at them and smiling. At that moment Andy Gillespie came back through the gate of the yard, almost walking right through Clare, and came at the children, his face red with anger.

'Where were you? what were you doing? Christ but it's bloody hard when you can't even say a few prayers for the holy souls without your own children disappearing on you and causing all sorts and kinds of trouble.' Richard and Mary Rose were taken firmly by an ear and led out through the side gate into the Church yard, Helen following; then they went back into the chapel for the fourth time.

During the early days of August, Clare did not come again to the lake. Once the children were discovered by their grandfather wandering about close to the sandy shore. Their father slapped each one of them, hard, across the backs of the legs and they were kept in the house all that long, hot, sad day. They kept their secrets, however, and the adults kept theirs.

One morning, very early, Helen woke believing she had heard sounds from the direction of the lake. Perhaps it was Clare. She slipped on a pair of runners and crept quietly out of her room, along the hallway and out the back door. She went very cautiously along the rough stone track towards the kesh; only a few birds could be heard, there was a coldness in the air, an intimation of things to come, a thin grey vapour hung on the lake. From behind a tree she watched her grandfather pulling the boat in on the shore and tying the rope around the rock. Perhaps he had been out fishing. There was no sign of Clare. She watched her grandfather go over to the kesh and walk out along it. She almost cried out to him to be careful, but she checked herself. He knelt down, reached in under the boards of the kesh; Helen saw him heave up the ropes with the plastic drum onto the boards of the kesh. He loosened something at the top, then, glancing round, he put his hand into his jacket pocket, took something out and put it in the drum, screwed back the top and lowered it all back down into the lake... Helen hurried back to bed.

The day was one of those late summer days when the sunshine hangs in the air like motes of straw-dust, a hot, dry day, the air thick as honey. The children moved about, lethargic, seeming always to be in somebody's way. The evening was exceptionally mild, the air sharpened to an especial clarity. Helen, Richard and Mary Rose were sent down to the parlour to play games; the adults were going to be busy and they were not to be disturbed. After several games of cards, all of which ended in squabbles, Helen announced that she could not stay in the house any longer. To the horror and thrilled dismay of the younger pair she hoisted the lower half of the window and climbed out, leaving it slightly open in case a rapid return was required.

She was in time to see her father and grandfather rowing out across the lake. It was late evening; she knew the men never fished so late; they seemed to be making straight across the inlet towards the kesh on the northern side. She watched for a while, then decided to go up onto the road and run quietly to see what they were doing. It was an unauthorised road, restricted to local traffic and to the border patrols. It was narrow and curved gradually upwards and around the lake, through trees. By the time Helen had come to the other kesh and had climbed down the embankment to the lake, the boat had gone again. There they were, just visible, almost back at the house.

Helen stood awhile, watching the lake. It was dreamily peaceful. In the distance somewhere a moorhen gulped. There were swallows swooping over the water. The reeds along the shore were perfectly still. If the giant otter really did exist, this was the perfect evening to encounter him. Soon Helen grew tired watching and turned for home.

As she climbed back up the embankment towards the road she heard the sound of an engine in the distance, heading up the road from the direction of her parents' house. No doubt it was an army patrol, one of those that passed up and round the lake irregularly. She did not want to be seen and she crouched into a small culvert beside the road. These were wicked men, she had been told, terrible monsters that would make away with anyone they caught wandering about. She hugged the sandy, gravelly wall of the culvert. There, by a small plastic bag carefully taped to a rock in the culvert, was an object that looked very like the kind of handset used with Richard's boat. The little antenna rose out of it and reached into the air.

Back at the house Helen's father was standing by a tree near the fence on his land. Old Tom Gillespie stood near him, a pair of binoculars focused on the patrol that was passing up along the road. Andy was holding a small transmitter in his left hand, his right hand poised over the button.

THE TARRED ROAD

Patcho Wheelan was big! heavy and cumbersome in his flesh, slow, deliberate, taciturn. The cheer-loud days of the great Joe Louis had gone by — he had tried a come-back, failed, and let the world down — but he had been the heavyweight champion of the world. Half in mockery, half in the certainty of his strength, our lumbering, heavy-treading labourer, Patcho Wheelan, had been nicknamed 'The Brown Bomber'.

'Bomber' was a word that seemed to encompass everything to do with power and bigness and aggression; and 'Brown' – well, in this case, because Patcho, like Joe Louis, was a fresh bog-earth brown all over. Brown from the harsh winds, from his long labours under our half-active sun, from the endless outdoors and from the long and suffocating heat of tar.

The Bomber worked on the roads. They were surfacing a stretch of road that began somewhere in the far, unreachable east and extended into an endless distance westwards. As far as the labourers knew, by the time they got to the furthest point west the road would have begun to curve round again until it was heading back due east, to join up with its origins, like the famous serpent that swallowed its own tail.

It was a slow job, tedious, exhausting, and thankless. As soon as the barrels and signs had been cleared away from one completed stretch of road they had to be set up again a hundred yards further on. The heaps of stones, the high green caravan, the painted tar barrels, the half-hearted warning signs, were all shifted like an old man with his crutches. At once boys left toe-prints in the still-soft tar; the iron rim of a cartwheel incised its furrows; a crack appeared, where the rains would gnaw and irritate. The world is salted by millions of gangs working in the heat and stench of tar to try to tie the world up firmly in a string of roads.

The Bomber had sworn, publicly, to do in the ganger. Whenever a car came picking its way through the loose stones and the barrels on the road, the Bomber would watch, taking in its shape, its power, its modernity, the wealth or the far-distant glories it suggested. He would watch until it had cleared the works and had disappeared around the first bend with a contemptuous dust-filled cock of its tail. And he would sigh, leaning over his muck-coated shovel.

When a woman cycled by, her long coat open over her knees, or her dress a little askew over the saddle of her bike, the Bomber would watch, allowing himself a rest, leaning on his spade, his great brown arms bunched under a dirty vest, an enigmatic half-smile on his face, and he would follow her movements until she, too, had disappeared, confused, into the distance. The Bomber never offered any comment on car or woman that passed, never entered into discussions on sex or pistons; he merely gazed, and sighed, and returned to the tar. It was all only dreaming, after all.

But dreams do not get the surface of a road levelled and tarred. The ganger was annoyed; how many man-hours were being lost over the days and weeks and months? and, being afraid of the Bomber's girth, he simply remarked, on an off-day, that the Bomber was a lecher. A lecher!

That evening, over a pint bottle of stout in Cafferky's bar, the Bomber asked The Mouth Horan what the word 'lecher' meant. Timothy Patrick Horan, who was known to quote occasionally some of the verses of the great poet Robert Service, and who, therefore, had acquired a reputation for learning among the members of the gang, took time to explain.

'The word "lecher",' he began, 'comes from an old Greek word, meaning sex. Today it comes from a Spanish or a German word, for milk. You see?'

'No.'

'Well. It's a word to do with sex, don't you know?'

'No.'

'Well, we all know sex is wicked, it's a sin. So that's it. Now you know.'

'No.'

'Well, Patcho, what more can I say? It's to have longings and imaginations for things beyond your reach. That's lechery. Things. Beyond your reach. Like sex, don't you know. Fornication, if you'll pardon the word. Carnal desires. Lust. That kind of thing.'

'What's milk got to do with it?'

'Milk?'

'Yes, you said German milk, or Spanish milk.'

'Oh no, Patcho, only the word, man, only the word. Comes from milk. Lewdness. A lecher is a fella drinkin' in the idea of sex, don't you know. A sex fiend, don't you see. A sex maniac. That's what a lecher is. There you have it. Now don't you know.'

'Milk! I hate milk!'

But the Brown Bomber had it. He was holding his bottle of stout in one big fist, spurning the use of a glass; he was leaning forward over the dark wooden top of the bar counter. Timothy Patrick Horan finished his speech and took a sip of his whisky and water. The Bomber nodded his rock of a head slowly, up, and down, up, and down; he looked at himself in the dust-smoked mirror at the back of the bar and, slowly raising the bottle to his mouth, he sucked away the contents. Milk! Then he crashed the bottle down onto the bar with such force that it shattered in his hand and flew about the pub in a hundred, black, murderous pieces.

'I'll do him in, the bugger,' the Bomber announced to the men, speaking slowly and carefully, as ever; 'I swear to the Sacred Heart of Jesus that I'll do the bugger in.'

He ordered another bottle of stout and watched the froth swelling in its brown-white beauty from the neck of the bottle. He wiped the froth with his big, brown finger, put the finger in his mouth and sucked it, offering Timothy Patrick a great wink as he did so. It was a long road. It twisted and turned.

There were several days of rain that week. The broken surface of the road breathed easily as the men stayed at home, watching out the windows, fixing drawers and door-latches, playing cards, arguing, listening to the wireless. In the late afternoon most of them put on their heavy winter coats and boots and hats, climbed on their bikes and worked their way through the rain to Cafferky's bar. Black days, long and grim and dulling. The high green caravan was pounded by rain and wind, water formed shivering puddles about its wheels. In the gloom of the little brown pub the gang brooded and drank, the Bomber sitting quietly on his bench, his eyes watching the concrete floor. Life is a long, black and white dream, black and white, tar and milk, a curiosity.

On Friday the rain eased and they were back on the road. The Bomber, handling spades, shovels, pickaxes and crow-bars, laughed out loud as he hefted them against rocks and stones. He eyed the ganger and laughed; it would be like killing cockroaches or beetles. The Bomber's great brown chest heaved against his dirty singlet, with its holes and its spatterings of tar. He lined up a rock, aimed at it and brought the spearpoint of the pick down at it; it split with a dull sound, its brains spilling, and he laughed.

Steam rose, the gang moved with black cans heavy with tar, filling in the places the sprayer missed, the edges, the hollows, the bumps. The road bubbled and spat. The men sweated. The tar was on their hands, on their clothes, on their faces, in their brains, and the Brown Bomber darkened imperceptibly. Rain came suddenly and the whole world hissed and steamed and darkened, too. The Bomber dropped his can and ran for the shelter of the blank gable wall of Carey's cowshed.

He shook the rain from his hair and ruffled his big hands through it. The wall was rough-stoned and white-washed, dirty from years of neglect, dark-green streaks of mould along it and black marks of animals where they had rubbed their hides dreamily along it. The Bomber moved his large hide over and back against the wall and grunted with satisfaction. The rain darkened the world and populated it with ghosts.

Then he saw the poster. It was pasted on one end of the gable wall, the top left-hand corner already peeling off and hanging down, sopping, and limp. The Bomber read slowly, aloud:

'The Wizard of Oz'.

'Friday night (tonight) at 7.30. Clandouglas Hall.

Admission two shillings and one and thruppence.

In glorious technicolour.'

The old Volkswagen van belonging to Pat the Brake Carter would collect the great spools of film from the afternoon train and drive back to Clandouglas where Cissie O'Hara would have the doors of the hall open at seven o'clock. The Bomber grinned with satisfaction. The pictures. Great! 'In glorious technicolour' — what the hell did that mean?

The two shilling seats in Clandouglas hall were kitchen chairs, twenty of them, placed in four rows in the centre of the hall. The one and thruppences were the forms fixed along the side walls. The Bomber sat with most of the others on the forms. You had to lean forward and look to your right or your left — depending on which side of the hall you were on — to see the screen. Carter had his projector up on a big table at the back of the hall, the large loudspeaker fixed on another table behind the screen. The Mouth had said the pictures would be in colour. The Bomber mocked him. Impossible, he said. Just black and white, and grey, as ever.

There was Pathe News. The Cock. Many of the men in the hall crowed along with it. The News. The unreal world. Out there. Then a short; a travel piece about cockatoos and banana trees and long, deserted beaches. Unreal. Non-existent. Boring. The Gang chattered softly amongst themselves. Then the film began and the Bomber guffawed aloud. The Metro Goldwyn Mayer lion was, as always, black and white. The Bomber put his two fingers in his mouth and whistled. Several people on the two shilling chairs looked at him, several on the forms laughed. The lion roared, three times. That was a good sign, a sign that this was going to be a good film.

A dull, country scene, farming folk, crude, a floppy dog, 'Toto', a young girl, a rickety house and farm, hens, eggs, a tyre hung from a tree to act as a swing. Familiar stuff, everyday, homely, dull, black and white, recognisable, boring! And when the girl began a song the shuffling and whispering of the men on the forms grew loud and intrusive. There were a few, half-hearted shushes from the chairs.

The Bomber bit into his six-penny bar of Cadbury's whole milk chocolate. He leaned back against the wall. He hated songs. Dean Martin always ruining the Jerry Lewis films. Dreamy, romantic nonsense. Nothing to do with anything. He could hear the splattering of rain on the galvanised roof of the hall. Not straining to look at the screen he was better able to pay attention to the words of the song. They began to move him.

Somewhere over the rainbow — a land not like this — a place where there would be no trouble. Once in a lullaby. A lovely, wistful melody. Stirring, heartfelt words. Birds fly over the rainbow. The Bomber knew a great deal about rainbows. Why, oh why, can't, I? He heaved a long sigh when the song ended. He noticed that everybody was listening intently, and watching, they were all moved by the song.

Gruffly he elbowed Vinsheen Hanratty in the ribs to make him laugh. Vinsheen shook his head at him, irritably. The Bomber looked at the screen again. Up there everything was in commotion; a storm rising rapidly, a 'twister' they called it, Dorothy Gale from Kansas and her little fluffy Toto caught in it — she was hurt — the house was flying through the air — it was falling, falling ... then stillness. Everybody in the hall gaped as the girl got up and moved slowly to open the cabin door. And then! oh then! the world outside ... oh God! oh then! ... The Brown Bomber, Vinsheen, The Mouth ... and ... the two shilling people, and all the one and thruppences, stepped out together into a world of vivid colours, the most startling and beautiful world anyone had ever seen. It was a living miracle, happening there in Clandouglas hall, before them; there were flowers everywhere, there were birds and skies and trees and houses, all in magnificent, delightful colour; there was music, and women dressed in pink, and wildly striped, wonderful Munchkins and and and soldiers, and bands, and dancers ... oh! the mind sang and the body strained and the chocolate melted in the Brown Bomber's fist.

Patcho Wheelan travelled every inch of the way along the unbelievable road constructed out of yellow bricks, not a trace of tar anywhere, side by side with Dorothy, and the tin man, and the scarecrow, and the cowardly lion; the Brown Bomber's mouth was wide open in astonishment and his breathing was hushed and gentle, his body rigid and tensed, his emotions caught in a whirlwind. Once he screamed in anger at the green, cackling face of the Wicked Witch of the West, and nobody noticed that it was the Brown Bomber who had screamed because each person thought that he was the one who had screamed. And when the picture stopped and the awful words 'The End' came up, they all sat stunned and silent until Cissie O'Hara clattered across the old wooden

floor of Clandouglas Hall and switched on the naked, dis-
heartening bulbs. They heard the rain, then, falling on the
galvanised roof, and when Cissie opened the heavy doors
they felt the cold demands of a black night waiting for them.

On Saturday evening, the Brown Bomber sat in a great
enamel basin in front of the hearth in his kitchen. He washed
himself thoroughly. He rubbed butter into all the places
where tar had congealed and he got a good deal of it off. He
scrubbed his body all over with a new bar of red Lifebuoy
soap; he lathered his hair with the soap several times, trying
to get the tar out. The stone flags of the kitchen floor were
splashed and greasy by the time he was finished.

He arrived late to eleven-thirty Mass in Clandouglas
Church, dressed in his navy-blue suit, the first time he had
worn it since the death of his mother years before. He wore
a white shirt, and a tie that was reasonably well knotted.
Father Henry had his back to the congregation; he was hard
of hearing, otherwise he would have noticed the silence in
the Church, the intake of breath, the whispering, the chuck-
les. In Clandouglas Church males take the benches to the left,
females take the right. Only fools and foreigners go into the
wrong side. The Brown Bomber walked as daintily as he was
able with his heavy, waddling gait, up the centre aisle to the
top bench. He was holding his cap in front of his crotch. He
genuflected, awkwardly, holding the end of a pew with his
left hand and blessing himself vaguely with his cap. Then he
pushed his way in amongst the women near the front. The
women giggled to themselves and buried their faces in their
prayerbooks.

But the Brown Bomber knew that he had waltzed through
a brightly coloured land, up the yellow brick road, towards
the Emerald City. There was a brilliant, shifting light, all
colours, streaming in through the rose window over the altar;
the harmonium struck up 'Somewhere Over the Rainbow'
and the choir of girls from Clandouglas National School

performed a Munchkin song. He knelt, praying fervently; he was a great hogweed among the daffodils, but he prayed to the wonderful wizard of the altar. Next Friday, he promised himself, he would dress in his best again and make his way to Clandouglas hall; it would be the second Friday of the month and he would present himself at the parochial dance and social to choose a bride to brighten up his days.

On Monday the sun shone on the tarred road. The Bomber presented himself, as usual, at the green caravan at the roadside and collected his tools. A gentle smile lit up his swarthy face, benevolence and cheer shone towards all. The gang chortled and sniggered amongst themselves and watched the Bomber take out an old and off-white handkerchief; he tied knots in each corner and fastened the handkerchief to his head. It would keep away the damaging rays of the midday sun; it would keep the tar from getting in among the ribs of his hair. He began shovelling stones into a wheelbarrow.

The raucous laughter of the ganger dropped the Bomber quickly out of his dream. Some of the men had been telling him of the Bomber's walk up the centre aisle at Sunday Mass, the way he preened himself before the women, the way he had his few ribs of hair plastered all to one side with an overdose of haircream. The ganger, a foreigner from the parish beyond the parish of Clandouglas, was a fool.

'I told you,' he said, loud enough for the Brown Bomber to hear, 'what did I tell you? He's a lecher, that's what he is, that slow-moving lazy old bastard. A lecher. No woman more beautiful than a tar barrel would look twice at him, God help us.'

With the speed of the Wicked Witch of the West astride her broom, the Brown Bomber, a storm, a twister, levelled the ganger with one resounding blow from his shovel.

A MESSENGER FROM THE GODS

Robert Emmet Lynchehaun walked down to the harbour every morning and every afternoon to watch the ferry coming in. It was mostly tourists who disembarked, Americans, Germans, Swedes ... and sometimes Irish. They came for the sun and for the beaches, where they could strip and lie in the heat and watch one another. Emmet waited beside the bus where he could observe without being noticed; when he was certain that everyone had disembarked he would talk to couples who were Irish, their hesitant movements giving them away, small flags on their rucksacks, or shamrocks embroidered on their bags. He would ask them quietly for news of home, speaking in that strange manner he had, right hand held over the mouth, almost smothering his words.

After he had seen them all off the ferry Emmet went into Vayena's bar and had one glass of beer before heading back to his house. The bus left Alepsiou and travelled four miles from the harbour to the town, Poli, that formed the business and holiday centre of the island. The road was narrow, risen dust from the wheels filled his mouth and settled on the dried-up fields and bushes. Emmet walked the four miles to Poli almost every day; he did not want to spend the few drachmas he had left on bus journeys. His tall, lean figure, dressed always in black — black trousers, black jacket, black waistcoat — had become a familiar sight along the road. He had picked up a few words in the weeks he had been waiting and enough basic phrases to order food and drink, to ask the man at the fishing port if there was a job for him yet.

'No, no, not yet, Ireland-man, soon, maybe, soon.'

Tassos would send word, he would send a messenger to Alepsiou to tell him to come; the fishing was not good, not yet, but soon, maybe, soon, when the weather changed, then there would be work, catching squid, cleaning the decks, cooking meals ...

'Soon, Ireland-man, soon now, the messenger come.'

On the morning of Tuesday, July 11th, Emmet was at the quay, waiting. The ship 'Athena' docked; he watched, hidden behind the bus. Among the passengers who disembarked he saw two young women who wore tee-shirts with 'Ireland' written in green across their backs. He watched them, savouring their northern accents, and then he approached, casually, helping them with the old woman who was offering accommodation.

'You're from the North of Ireland, then?'

'Yes, we are; I'm Deirdre, this is Maeve. And you? you're from the North as well, aren't you?'

Emmet brought them to Vayena's and bought beers. They were going to stay for a few days, then move on to another of the islands. They were in their twenties, pretty, and he relaxed in their company.

'And how are things in the North these days?'

'As bad as ever,' Deirdre said. She told of the troops and the police, the ambushes, the bombs.

'Are ye Republicans, then?'

'Of course,' said Maeve with animation. 'Aren't you?'

'Yes, yes, I suppose I am. But it's been a few months since I was home and I suppose you get different ideas out here.'

'What do you mean, different ideas? Isn't it the same all the time, England the oppressor, Ireland the slave, never at peace until all her children are free? What can be different about that fact, no matter what part of the world you're in?'

'Well,' Emmet answered, hesitantly, 'I don't know, really. There's something static about all that Cathleen stuff, it's been like that for centuries, and I see no change; out here the place is full of myths, myths attached to places and things, but always changing, Apollo, Zeus, Aphrodite, you know, all of that; even the boat you came out on was called *Athena*, goddess of wisdom. You see old people here and you think of Zeus and Hera, moving, changing, living myths. They seem to shift with the times, move as the people move. Anyway, I just don't know. But I'm writing about it, you know, the myth thing; and my own experiences back home will come into it, a sort of a novel really, trying to make some sense of it all.'

Deirdre and Maeve were both silent, looking at their beers.

'By the way,' he added; 'you don't happen to know a chap called Connor McLure, from Newry, do you? He's sort of squat, a well-built fellow, dresses in black, like myself, but he's got a great fright of white hair; looks a bit like a pint of Guinness.'

'No,' said Deirdre, looking to Maeve; 'no, I can't say that we know him.'

'And you didn't see anybody like that around Piraeus by any chance, did you? Getting a ferry or anything?'

'No, there was nobody like that while we were there.'

Again there was silence between them.

'Listen, thanks for the beers,' Maeve said at last, 'and maybe we'd better be going. That old lady is expecting us up at her house. Is there anything happening on this island? Where's the best place for a bit of fun?'

He told them about Poli, the restaurants, the seafront, the disco. They arranged to meet at one of the restaurants and then go together to the disco. He was delighted, it was time to break the rope of isolation that bound him to the island, like Prometheus lashed to his rock, if only for one day.

Emmet walked back to the house; it was after noon and the heat weighed heavily on the island. He had made notes already, notes carefully hidden under loose floorboards of the house. Names, even, and dates, phrases taken down verbatim. Soon, perhaps, soon, he would get down to it. Soon, when all of it seemed to have taken shape and order in his mind. Soon. But not just yet. Not until he was sure that the messenger had come and gone, or that no messenger was ever going to come.

In the meantime there were the love lyrics to be working on, the poems that gave him some relief. On the banks of the river Boyne he had made love, and there were seasons then when the whole of life seemed to be as ordered as that river, the wild duck coming at the nub of Winter, the primroses daring the world along hidden cracks in the soil at the lift of Spring, the basin filling with floodwaters, then easing back into quietness. Gráinne she called herself, but he preferred to think of her as Grace; the grace of her white, cool limbs, the grace of the gift of herself to him, the truth of her flesh and of her words, the way her long fingers moved through his black, shocked hair, drawing out the disorder and anguish from his brain. He waited now for the breath of inspiration, for a messenger from the Gods, to give him words that would hold her near him once again.

There was a sudden scattering of noise outside; Emmet leaped from his chair and moved in behind the door; he was panting, holding his tall body tightly against the wall. Then he heard loud laughter and voices; he glanced out; there was a group of Germans passing on the road. He watched them, their certainty, their fuss and bickering over a can of Coke, their definition, their certain familiarities. They moved on down the road towards Poli.

Emmet, realising that the lyric mood had passed, went out into the day, locking windows and door, locking in the words. He took a path that led over a hill towards the sea.

Everything was stilled under the heat; he could imagine why they had given a name to the sun, why it had become a living God to the people here. He took off his jacket, threw it over one shoulder. If only Grace would come ... She would have got his letter some time ago, long enough to have her get a flight and then a boat to the island. But perhaps they were watching her home, too, and perhaps even her mail?

He watched a hawk soaring over scrub on the side of the hill. It circled, its focus narrowing, then dipped and dived, its claws stretched out beneath it. Then it rose again and he could see a tiny life pierced through by those claws. He screamed at the bird, flung his arms in the air and ran forward, swirling his jacket about over his head. The bird, startled, dropped its prey and flew swiftly off over the hill. Emmet heard the thud the falling creature made on the ground. He ran to find it. It was a young hare, there were blood marks where the claws had penetrated the flesh, it was still breathing, but its body was twisted and its eyes looked up with terror at this new hunter.

Emmet longed for the definition and power of a pistol in his hand, its firmness, its weight, the ease with which it allows decisions to be made and carried out, the finality of its statement, its immediacy in the ordering of life. But he had no pistol, there were only the stones scattered on the hillside; he put the hare down, carefully, then lifted a heavy stone and held it high.

The experience left him weak and angry. He sat down a while, the sky above him cruel now in its heat, the ground harsh and unwelcoming, the world divided into hunter and hunted, the gods gathered in their halls, hatching mischief. If only Grace would come ... if only!

He went on again, over the hill, down a slope towards the sea. This was a quieter part of the island, known to the locals and a few regular visitors. There was a small beach, the water was clear, the sand clean and white. He sat on the rocks at one end of the beach, took off his waistcoat and shirt, spread them out behind him. Then he took off his trousers and pants and made a sudden rush, naked, into the water. It was cool and refreshing, and he swam happily for a time, the water cleansing and easing him, caressing his tense and tiring body.

All at once, as if a cloud had come between him and the sun, he shivered; someone was watching him; he had that familiar sensation of fear chilling his spine; up on the low cliffs above the beach? He jerked his head up to look; he could not be sure; had he caught a glimpse of someone moving away? or was it just a shadow on the cliff top accentuated by the suddenness of the glare in the sky when he looked up? In spite of the sun he felt cold. He pulled on his clothes over his wet body and headed back over the hill.

He stopped in Alepsiou to have his lunch, a can of beer, a few nuts and a cheap sandwich. As he sat on the terrace, once again he had the feeling of being watched. He glanced around him with as much unconcern as possible ... but he saw nothing, no one new or strange or expected. He finished his beer and went down to the harbour. There was a ferry due in at three o'clock but when he came to the harbour he was surprised to see a ship pulling out; the 'Hermes,' he was told, had been put on as an extra because of the number of tourists wanting to come out to the islands. The 'Hermes' had come in shortly after noon.

The rest of the day stretched out hot and empty before him. He went back to the house and lay down in his room. He dozed, strange images surfacing to disturb him. His father — those lemon-yellow gloves he wore when he was pottering around the greenhouse, how they had always distressed Emmet, that perfectly arranged rockery, the immaculate rows of flowers in the garden, the perfect order of the green-house, the irritating accuracy and clicking of the secateurs; such pointless order in a world of total disorder had always disturbed him. And how his father would sit, at precise moments, on the garden chair to wait for each passing train on the Belfast/Dublin line, how he sat and watched its coming, its passing and its going, watching something real come noisily into a wasted life and leave as noisily as it had come.

Emmet fell into a sweating, restless sleep. He was back again in Belfast on that evening when he had done his duty, as he was ordered to, when he held the pistol, (how easy it had been,) to flag down the van, to take it in along the unlit side street, to take out the named one from among his fellows as they drove home from work, how easy to put a gun to the back of the neck, to pull the trigger. Emmet had known no fear, not then, no hesitation, he had not even begun to sweat. He was perfect. A born killer, a hunter. It was only later that the slumping down at his feet of the suddenly heavy body had begun to haunt him, falling against his legs and knocking him backwards, off balance. He knew the man was dead before he hit the street but that thud of the skull against asphalt echoed in his brain like a slow, slow drum.

He came awake with a start. There was someone outside. He was sure of it. The footsteps were cautious, hesitant, but they were there. He was suddenly cool again. There was no fear. He moved quickly to his position behind the door, where he could not be seen from the window. He picked up the fire iron that he kept ready for such a moment. He would not be taken as easily as he had taken his prey barely a year before. The footsteps were outside the door. There was a timid knock and Emmet faltered. He would not knock, when he came, he would come unannounced, without preamble, without words.

'Who's there?'

A man's voice outside murmured something in Greek. Emmet relaxed, put down the bar and opened the door. There was an old man there with a written message he handed to Emmet.

'Tomorrow morning, Poli, harbour, 6 in the clock, come,

work. Tassos.'

The old man was astonished when Emmet burst out laughing and grabbed him by the shoulders. He brought him inside and took a bottle of white wine from the fridge. He poured them each a glass and laughed again. The only word spoken was 'Prosit!' There was much laughter, a lot of smiles.

In the early evening Emmet set out on the four mile walk to the fishing village. The sky was still blue and clear but the heat had begun to ease; God was in his heaven, all was right. He sat on the terrace of one of the restaurants crammed with tourists and ordered a glass of ouzo and a saucer of pistachio nuts. Life was good, and soon, very soon, Grace would come. Tomorrow he would be on the sea and the money would be gathering. Deirdre and Maeve arrived and they all dined together, Emmet feeling happy to fling the last of his money into a good evening. They drank two bottles of wine. The lights came on about the harbour; the rigging on the yachts, the pleasure craft and the fishing boats made soft tinkling sounds in the evening breeze. Like a flock of cows on an Alpine pasture, he announced. They ordered Metaxa, rough, local brandy. Then Maeve and Deirdre left him, saying they would join him later at the disco. He drank heavily. He was celebrating.

Later in the evening he was seen at the 'Elektra' club, dancing to the loud disco music, dancing alone. The music died at two a.m. sharp and he was seen to leave, still alone, and very drunk. At two o'clock the following afternoon his body was discovered, naked, at the secluded beach behind the hill; he was lying, face down among the rocks, one small, neat bullet hole in his temple.

LEO

Leo spent a lot of time in the shed. People never knew what he was doing in there. People had theories. People go round having theories. Life goes round and round. Leo never volunteered any information. Out of a natural, island discretion, nobody presumed to ask Leo what he was doing in the shed. How can you ask a man in the prime of his manhood:

'Hey, there, Leo, what do you be doin' in there in th'oul shed, wha'?'

It was dark in the shed. There was only one, very small, square window in the back wall, long grown opaque from the accumulation of dust, cobwebs, the mummified bodies of spiders, the shells of flies, the wings of moths and butterflies. Along one wall stood large wooden grain bins from the days when the land was farmed and there were cattle and horses to feed. Oats, barley, rye ... The air of the shed was thick with dust and memories. The great wheel of life grown rusty, little specks of rust lay about the floor. A single, weak light-bulb hung unshaded from the ceiling.

It was after midnight. A storm rushed and raged over the island, rattling the bolts and window-joists, driving ever deeper into the soil the roots of fuchsia and furze-bush. Leo closed the back door of his house and stood a moment gazing up towards the impenetrable sky; there were no stars, nor were there lights anywhere to reflect off the low, black clouds. Leo shivered and ran quickly across his back yard, flashing his torch, outlining before him the box-like shape of his shed. Hurriedly he went inside, closed the door behind him, bolted it and switched on the bulb.

Things scurried away from the intruder; there were rustling sounds from corners, things barely glimpsed vanished at once into holes, under skirting-boards, between slits of the ceiling beams. Leo leaned against the door and listened to the sounds of the storm outside.

He was tall, thin and long as a fishing-rod. He had red hair which was already thinning out. He wore a many-coloured knitted woollen cap which people had rarely seen him without. Leo's many-coloured dreamcoat. It seemed an essential part of his shape, an extension to his head, a full-stop and exclamation mark at the end of the sentence that was Leo.

Leo lifted the lid of one of the grain-bins and left it lying back against the dusty wall. He went to the door, checked that it was locked, then switched off the light. Now he was in a darkness within the world darkness. He stood for a while, savouring that darkness. The winds continued, the rain came in squalls, spluttering comfortably against the window. The mighty ball that was the globe rolled on and on through space. Leo stood perfectly still. Very soon little rustling sounds began once more. Leo could see nothing, not even a vague outline of the shape of the window. He sighed with satisfaction. Something brushed lightly against his shoe; he did not move. This was a familiar darkness. He appreciated it.

At last he stretched out his two arms and groped his way forward, feeling for the wood of the open bin. When he found it he climbed inside, his long, thin body flowing over the edge of the bin like a stream of water over a low barrier or rocks.

He stood upright on the floor of the bin for a long moment, relishing a surge of satisfaction. Then he lowered himself, slowly, until he was squatting on the wooden floor, his knees pressing against the front of the bin, his spine against the back. Again he paused, in anticipation, and then, holding the lid of the bin with his two hands he bent his head down onto his knees, lowering the lid as he did so. He slipped his left hand down and lowered the lid the rest of the way with his right hand. The lid fell with a soft clunk as he jerked away his hand. Now if he raised his head it butted against the lid of the bin. He breathed out, relaxing. He was in a deeper darkness within the shed's darkness that was itself inside the great world darkness. He blinked his eyes rapidly several times, then closed them, gently; finally he furrowed his brow and wrinkled up his cheeks and the bridge of his nose, conscious that the eyes were shut tight. He was in his private darkness now, within the deep darkness of the bin, inside the shed's particular darkness that was contained in the great world darkness. Within the dark, unfathomable waters of creation.

He breathed in the musty scent of the bin through his nostrils. At the back of the bin there was an inch of space between bin and wall. There were several air-holes there. His long, supple body settled easily into its foetal shape. Soon he would sleep. Soon, perhaps, he would slip through into that darkness that would lead him out beyond all darknesses into the world of dreams. Tiny teeth gnawed fretfully at soft wood somewhere on the base of the bin. Leo did not mind. The cap on his head was warm and soothing as a parent's caress. He heard, faintly, a small flutter of wings in some far-off darkness. He could not hear the storm. The sound and motion of the great grinding wheels of life had stilled. He was dry. He slept.

~

Leo's boat was drawn up on a grass bank above the pier. It was small, but effective, tied to the earth by ropes attached to large stones sunk in the ground on either side. The oars he left in the bottom of the boat, life on the island still being innocent as the days before first confession. The outboard engine he stored in the cabin of the 'Maria Goretti', Peter Cafferky's half-decker, where it was kept dry from the rains which made dirty pools in the bottom of the boat. If the 'Maria Goretti' happened to be at sea, then Leo simply rowed to and from his fishing-grounds.

Leo came from his house at the top of the village down to the pier, by bike. He had an old Rudge, ancient of days, strong as a cart-horse, black and matt as night. It was without brakes. Like the earth herself. The bike exhaled as Leo approached, it panted, trembling in its place, anxious for the off. Leo, it could be said, melded the bike to his body rather than mounted it. He set off at a blistering pace, his aim being to freewheel as far as possible from the top of the road to the pier. Head down, woollen cap at point, long body hunched forward like a jockey's, he made for the pier with such unity of purpose as brooked no hindrance, accepted no greeting, admitted no obstacle.

Leo let the Rudge lie where it halted, on the ground, with little rosaries of seaweed among the salt-burned grasses and the half-naked clumps of sea-thrift. Little eyes watched from the brown and yellow leaves of sea-wrack. Palping shapes under the surface of the low-tide mud heaved slowly as they waited. There was no sign of the 'Maria Goretti'.

Leo drew from a canvas shopping-bag his daffodil-yellow oilskin suit. Trousers. Jacket. He turned from the boat and moved down to the shore, searching the silt for tracks of foot or hoof of something risen from the sea that morning. There was nothing. A soft, belching sound from the mud further out caught his attention; there was a bubbling under the black filth and Leo grinned; something forming there, he knew, obscene and lewd and gut-ugly. Real. In the blackness.

He loosened the boat from the rocks, then lifted one side and rocked it to empty out the gathered pool of water. There were six tiny green crabs left on the bottom of the boat, scuttling hither and yon now that their world had so suddenly flowed away from them.

'Ha-ha!' said Leo with great satisfaction. 'It's begun!' and he looked up at the dark sky, still heavy with clouds. 'Raindrops, that form into little green crabs to haunt the bottom of my boat.'

He ran the boat over the grass, the small stones, the ooze, the silt, into the quietly lapping water of the harbour. It was like running a bicycle on the road to mount it. He leaped in and quickly crushed the little green crabs into small heaps of green and white dust. Then he sat to the oars. Leo, rowing his fourteen-foot fibre-glass boat, looked like an extension of that boat, like a mast, yellow-sailed, bunting-topped, straining to the voyage. He rowed strongly, out from calm waters into the channel where the swell ran high after yesterday's storms.

Out beyond the breakers the Atlantic heaved and wallowed. Leo and his boat lolled and bobbed in perfect harmony with the ocean. Leo shipped his oars, took out a sandwich from its newspaper wrapping and chewed contentedly. Then he lowered a long line overboard, allowing the dozen feathers attached to sink far down into the darkness of the sea. The frenzied shoals of mackerel would be going by. Nourishment. A life-line. Leo gazed into the water, and waited.

After a while the 'Maria Goretti' materialised out of a darkening afternoon, its engine chugging like an old man coughing through the night. As it approached, Peter Cafferky cut the engine and emerged from the steer-house to wave to Leo.

'Leo!'
'Peter!'
'Want the outboard?'
'Nah!'
Pause.
'Taking?'

'Th'odd wan!'

'You'll needs be gettin' a jerk into yourself — thon sky's a treacherous-lookin' hoor!'

A wave of the hand.

Dismissed.

Peter went back inside and the engine vomited twice, then caught. Sitting in the stern, untangling ropes, was Patsy Joe MacManus. His one good eye watched Leo, his old creosoted face set in its perpetual, inane grin. Leo saw the good eye, but his gaze fixed itself, as always, on the terrible socket of the empty eye, its purple weal, the red veins, the running soreness of it. All at once there was a ferocious tug on Leo's line. He began to haul.

Leo's heart pounded. He forgot, at once, all about the 'Maria Goretti', about Peter Cafferky and Patsy Joe MacManus. This was no mackerel passing; even with every feather taken the weight and drag would not be so great as this. The afternoon darkened. A hand-scattering of raindrops was flung against him. He held the line with both hands and pulled, standing up on the boards of the boat. A great dark shape grew visible, plumping the surface of the water, a thick, black shape, large as a seal, large as a man. It rolled back down into the darkness of the water. Leo, keeping the line quietly taut, let it play out of his hands with the creature.

'Hah!' he shouted. 'Cloven-foot! Is it you?'

Down, down, down went the creature, down went the line, running steadily out through Leo's hands, burning his palms, until the coil of it in the boat was growing dangerously small. Then, all at once, the line went slack.

Leo hesitated. There was a sudden screech of wind from nearby. He was leaning over the gunwale now, watching down into the green darkness of the water. The boat leaned with him. Leo began to pull, slowly, evenly. The line came with him. He pulled more quickly. Either the monster had got away or it was rising rapidly towards the surface. Leo sat down, still pulling. Suddenly there was a great swelling of the water and the dark shape of the fish appeared for a moment in the blackness before bursting over the surface and crashing sickeningly against the side of the boat.

The rain began, cold and loud, and the universe darkened. There was a great clamouring in Leo's ears and then the creature surfaced again, on the other side of the boat, a great tree-trunk rising out of the blackness, red eyes flaring, jaws gaping, coming at him with a speed and violence he could not withstand. The line snapped somewhere under the boat; Leo was jerked backwards and at that moment the creature struck the boat a terrible crash. Leo was tossed sickeningly into the sea.

He sank into a sudden, total silence, into a darkness that was seething with motion and power, he flailed his arms, he kicked with his legs, the daffodil oilskins were cumbersome, he shucked off his jacket, the trousers were filled with the ocean, he was sinking, he brought up his knees, he lowered his head, he was in a darkness within a darkness, he got the trousers off and he kicked, gasping and burning back to the surface of the sea.

Like a seal's his head appeared into the rain and the agony of the afternoon. The boat was bobbing, upright and careless, not far from him. He swam towards it. It was difficult to make any progress in that deadly swell. For long moments the boat disappeared from his view in some deep sea valley, only to surface again and rise high on the crest of a wave above him. Leo swam, closing slowly on the old boat, closing, closing; then he was very near, he closed his eyes, stretched out his two arms before him to touch the wooden comfort of his boat.

~

It was several days before Leo's boat came gently in on a high tide and beached itself on Dugort Strand. One side was severely staved in, as if it had received a vicious blow. There were no oars. The search for Leo continued for many days. The jacket of a daffodil-yellow oilskin suit was found on rocks miles away, under the high cliffs of Achill Head. The oilskin trousers were found, washed into a cove on Clare Island. The Air Corps helicopter continued its search, flying low along the base of the cliffs, hovering over the inaccessible landfalls strewn with the sea's flotsam. People walking on shores and beaches were warned. People had theories. There were no facts.

~

Leo woke in his own darkness. He was stiff and sore. He opened his eyes, slowly, painfully. The darkness remained as deep. He lifted his hand from his foetal position and tried to shove, upwards. It was difficult. He had been in this position for such a long time. There was a smell of sea-wetness, his body felt damp and cold. He was shivering. He pushed again, with the top of his head, raising his hands to help, trying to straighten out his legs. Push. Push. Push. Gradually the wooden lid began to give way. It screamed as Leo pushed his long body out of the darkness. Leo's eyes hurt at the brightness of the shed. The door was open and the sunlight from the world was flooding in. It made the shed look different, clean, and abused.

Leo, standing in the bin, stretched himself, easing out his limbs, his bones, his muscles. He was very wet. He raised his hand to his head and was surprised that his woollen many-coloured dream-cap was no longer there. The air of the shed was dense with pollens and dusts and memories. The cement floor was thick with the flotsam and jetsam of years. When Leo came out into the day his brain was clogged with dust. His eyes smarted, he sneezed loudly and often.

He went indoors and changed and filled his canvas shopping

bag with what he needed for the day. Then he came back out, mounted his bike and cycled through the gate of his yard. At that moment Betty-Ann McNulty was walking by, two plastic bags in her hands.

'Lovely day, Mrs McNulty,' Leo called, surprising himself.

The old woman did not turn her head; she stalked by as if Leo did not exist.

'Up yours too!' Leo murmured and he set off at his usual breathtaking pace down the long slope to the pier.

The 'Maria Goretti' was just a few yards out when Leo got off his bike; the half-decker was heading out to sea. The morning was being warmed by a lustrous sun, the sea sparkled invitingly, the lapping of the waves was soothing and melodious. Leo cycled all the way out over the holes and bumps and broken stones to the end of the pier. The half-decker was passing just beyond him.

'Hey! Youse!' he shouted.

Peter Cafferky was standing in the wheel-house, gazing at the open sea ahead of him. Leo whirled his arms about wildly. Peter did not turn his head. Patsy Joe MacManus was standing in the stern, gazing back up over the fields and meadows towards the village. His thumbs were hooked into his braces high over the lobster-pot of his belly.

'Hey! Patsy! Are yiz dead or what are yiz?' Leo yelled.

The half-decker grunted and farted its way past the end of the pier. Leo hopped about, waving his arms and shouting. Patsy did not turn his head. Then the half-decker veered to ease its way out into the open sea and he saw Patsy's jellied eye, its empty socket, its purple-coloured weal. That awful eye seemed to stare right through Leo's body. He stood still and watched the little cache of hopeful gulls that followed the 'Maria Goretti's' wake into the demands of another day.

Leo left the bike in the soft grass near his boat. From his canvas shopping-bag he drew out his daffodil-yellow oilskin suit. He turned from the boat and moved down to the shore, searching the silt for unusual foot or hoof-marks. He was gratified to see two shapes in the mud, a step distant from each other, like boot-prints, going deep into the silt, between high-water mark and the stones of the shore.

He loosened the boat from the rocks, then lifted it high on one side to rush out the pools of water. There were six tiny green crabs left in the bottom of the boat, scuttling hither and yon now that their world had so suddenly flowed away from them.

'Ha-ha!' said Leo, with a grunt of satisfaction, 'so! at long last, it's begun.'

FREE RANGE

Reynolds was sitting in a crotch of the sycamore tree. It was late summer, the leaves were plentiful, he could see without being seen. Blackbird. The keen eye. Over his high back wall he could look down onto the keyhole cul de sac where Jonathan Hayes was washing his car again. Third time this week he had washed it, hosing it down, rubbing it with a damp rag, going over it all again and again with a dry cloth, polishing, rubbing, testing. Watching his reflection in it. Wearing it out. But Reynolds was high, holding himself tight in against the bole of the tree, his arms around it, his legs dangling. There was scarcely any wind, the tree was still, unresponsive.

Reynolds looked over the walls on either side of his back yard; not one of the neighbouring women lay out today, basking in the sunshine, topless, bikinied, exposing themselves to the sky. To the keen eye.

Val Mulgrew, blue-suited, red tie, blue shirt, gloves for the steering wheel, came out of his house in the keyhole cul de sac, shouted something to Jonathan Hayes, waved his keyring with its chains and keys, like a dog-leash, in the air. As he approached the car it flashed its lights, a dog wagging its tail in recognition. Then it barked three times. Sharply. Val Mulgrew got into his car. The car moved away with a quiet growl of restrained power.

Reynolds, a few months back, had had to get rid of his old dog, Prince; too many of the neighbours had objected to its barking. The poor silly animal had been used to other poor silly animals prowling near the yard and Reynolds had encouraged his barking. But Prince had presumed to bark at Mrs Quinn-O'Meara from number 42 The Orchards and at Mrs Quinn-O'Meara's young cowboy sons, Derek and Austin, and so ...

Reynolds began to climb down slowly, holding carefully to the branches, easing his body down, limb by limb, to the earth. When he touched ground, like Daedalus, he straightened himself up, holding his kidneys with both hands, stretching himself backwards, loosening the old bones and joints.

A hen clucked peacefully among the scutch grasses near the shifting borders of the tree's shadow. Reynolds dived: an egg! white and perfect and warm, a delicate feel to it against the hard skin of Reynolds's palm. He walked across the yard into his house and left the egg on a draining-board by the sink. That was seven hen-eggs already today, as well as three duck-eggs and two goose-eggs: not bad, not bad at all. Reynolds came to the back door again and looked out over his kingdom.

There were fowl everywhere, picking, pecking, clucking, chortling, floating themselves about on the worn out earth of his back garden. The three walls that enclosed the garden were topped by several feet of chicken-wire, the wooden posts that held them were rotting and leaning all over the world, but effective still. The old huts and sheds at the end of the garden were falling apart, too, they hadn't been painted for many, many years; but they served! They formed an oasis of colour and individuality, their interior darknesses rich with the deposits and the memories of his fowl.

Cochin China and Brahma Pootra were brooding in a group in a warm pool of sunshine; soft bitches, these, but good layers and excellent brooders. Reynolds had Partridge, Buff and Cinnamon Cochin China, coarse ladies all, tough and boney to the palate, but constant, will sit and sit and sit, their small eggs tasty. With them were the brown Brahmas, dull birds, but sitters, too, mutterers, hatchers, egg-givers. Generous, like Reynolds, to a fault.

Reynolds hitched up the straps of his braces with his thumbs, let them snap back against his chest. There was no better judge of an egg than Reynolds, nobody had ever come so close to understanding the language of fowl, their habits, their needs, their urgencies. As he walked slowly round his demesne Reynolds rattled off the individual names for his hens, Nancy, Kelly, Mitsy, Grace, Helen, Sarah, Joanna, Clare ... He never got them wrong, never, and he knew their surnames, too: Langshan, Plymouth, Dorking, Leghorn, Minorca, Andalusian, White-face, Wyandotte. The best families only. No blow-ins. Pedigree.

There clucked Dame Hilda Orpington herself, handsome in her lustrous black gown, large and self-opinionated and delicate when she chose to be. Dame Hilda had gone a little past her best, Reynolds knew, but he could not see his way, not yet, to tapping her lovely head against the stump of the old beech tree. Clunk! and that reproachful eye, Judas! Brutus! after all the years of faithful service!

Reynolds paused outside the red shed, the one he had painted years ago with the colour they used on the post-boxes in the days when the sun shone and the warm afternoons lasted for ever. In those days this little lane was a country lane, you could hear a cart come trundling up the hill for a half-hour before it turned the corner onto the lane, you could hear the lark and the cuckoo and the corncrake, long ago, in the days of our poverty, when we took life gently and laid our own, slow, eggs. Heather Hill it was then, lovers' fields and skulking places, with just three cottages scattered among small meadows and smaller gardens, vegetable patches, water-barrels, hen-runs, gates. Now only the Reynolds cottage was left, the city having flopped its heavy body down to brood and stretched its flashy, nether parts out in all directions round it. Heatherfield Heights had become a fashionable neighbourhood, Heatherfield Walk, Heatherfield Avenue, Heatherfield Close, The Glebe, The Orchards ... And Heatherfield Park where the Reynolds cottage was an eyesore among the neo-Georgian squares and the neo-Tudor patches of the new estates.

Inside the door of the red shed Reynolds kept his shotgun, cleaned, primed, and ready. It had served him well against fox and badger, he had even shot to earth a harrier that had thrown too keen an eye over his fowl. Pigeons, too, he had taken out of the sky, thieves that would come and steal his grain, or dare to dally in little love-rushes with members of the Reynolds fowl harem. Today he had seen a couple of magpies perch high in the branches of the sycamore; they would be after the small eggs of the Brahma or the Cochin. They would even rip to bits the little honeyed softness of the chicks if they got a chance! It would be a grace to shoot them into Hell, to let off the great shout of the gun among the strained and crooked-eyed people of Heatherfield Heights.

Reynolds reached his hand inside the door, into the hen-fragrant darkness of the shed; his fingers found the cold clean line of the barrel, his hand moved down slowly and caressed the broadening stock, its polished wood, its delicate, sensitive grain. He sat down, then, just outside the door of the shed, on an old wooden chair, and waited. The high reaches of the sycamore tree were free for the magpies; let them come, now, let them come!

Reynolds settled himself on his chair, stretched out his legs over the shit-blackened ground in front of him, smacked his lips together several times to join in the muttering and murmuring contentment of his fowl, and let his eyes roam over the little area of blue sky he could see. He had tried to come to terms with Heatherfield Heights, goodness knows but he had given it his best shot.

He called on Mr and Mrs Jonathan and Sylvia Hayes soon after they had settled into number 34 The Glebe. He gathered together one dozen of his finest eggs, white and brown; he spat on them and rubbed and polished them to a fine sheen — (the bringing of dirty eggs to any house being a cause of deep disgrace) — he laid them out in a basket floored with clean straw, he shaved himself and put on his best jacket. He drew the line at a tie, a tie was for God alone, and that only on Christmas Day and on Resurrection Sunday. He presented himself one Sunday morning at number 34 The Glebe. He knocked loudly on the door.

There was no answer. Then Reynolds noticed a small bell-push. He pushed it. He could hear the buzz from deep inside the house. He was startled when a voice, tinny and crackling and female, hissed like an angry goose at him from a small contraption to the side of the door. He looked at it for a while, then he pressed the bell again.

The young woman opened the door. Pretty. Very, verrrry pretty. Like a doll. Neat.

'Yes?'

'Hello there! I'm Reynolds. From beyond. And I wish you a hearty welcome to Heather Hill.'

A nice, dark line down between the breasts that definitely draws the eyes into warmth, a heaving warmth, downy, fleshy and soft to the touch, I would say.

'Jonathan! Jonathan!'

She turned back to him, smiling, not quite sure what to say next. His boots were boots. There would be dirt. And his trousers looked like sacks. There would be dirt. And his shirt, stained everywhere, a stain with a shirt on it, it would smell. You could see a gathering of hairs, grey hairs, tufted, where the collarless shirt opened. There would be smells. 'Jonathan!'

A tall, well-built young man came to the door and the woman moved back a little.

'He says he's from here and he wants to welcome us!'

'Oh! Oh yes. That's nice. Come in! Come in!'

'I brang some eggs. Fresh eggs. You know. Not from them forced sheds where they torture the chickens. These are real. Free range. Like meself. A present.'

'How nice! Come on in! have a drink!'

Dressed in a track-suit he is, ready for a race-meet or some such. At twelve o'clock. But a drink now, yes, why not?

They led the old man into their new drawing-room. There was a large, light-tan-coloured suite of furniture, deep, dangerous-looking, leather. Reynolds looked down into the armchairs and decided against them. He might not surface. There was an enormous painting over the fireplace, a seascape, blue, and dark-blue and white, waves, and sky and foam. There was an artificial fire in the fireplace, flames that seemed to reach and shift and move, but that didn't, really. And everything gleamed, and shone, and dazzled.

'Eggs!'

'Oh yes, thanks, thanks very much. Sylvia, darling, will you take these out to the kitchen, pet? My name's Jonathan, by the way, Jonathan Hayes, and this here is my wife, Sylvia, Sylvia Johnston. And you are ... ?'

'Reynolds. I'm Reynolds. Are you married, then?'

'Married? Us? Oh yes, I see. Yes, yes, yes, we're married all right. Sylvia just wants to keep her own name, you know? Feminism and all that sort of thing. Mr Reynolds, it's nice to meet you. Would you like a drink?'

Jonathan followed Sylvia out of the room and into the kitchen where they closed the door, softly. They giggled into each others' faces. Sylvia put the eggs straight into a binliner and put the binliner in the bin outside the back door. Too strong, these eggs, too strong, if they're free-range eggs. Dangerous.

Reynolds remained standing in the drawing-room. He could hear a faint ticking sound from the fireplace. The carriage-clock on the mantelpiece was working all right but he could not hear any ticking sound from it. He was nervous. Cold. He thought he'd skip it, out the door ... Jonathan came back in.

'Sherry be all right?'

'Sherry?'

'Will you take a glass, darling?'

They had three glasses of sherry. Reynolds took the glass in his big fist and swallowed down the liquid at one gulp. Jonathan looked at Sylvia. Sylvia turned away. There was no fire she could poke at. Jonathan filled Reynolds's glass again. Again he tossed it back at one gulp. Sylvia went out, 'to put the kettle on.' Jonathan had nothing to say.

'Well, thanks. I'll be gettin' back now. I hope you'll be very happy here. Whenever ye want a real egg just give me a shout. Nothing like an egg. It's a true thing. Got all the world in it. All creation. Perfect. I'm over your garden wall. There beyond. Just that. So. I'll be goin' so.'

Jonathan ushered him out, ushering with him a vague smell of hens and eggs and darkness. Jonathan poured his sherry back into the bottle and went to rejoin Sylvia in the kitchen.

Deep within his dream now, under the creative embrace of the sun, Reynolds was on his hands and knees on the dirtied earth, scrabbling slowly around after a great Sebastopol Goose. She was a famed, prolific goose, almost as old as Reynolds himself, and a good deal wiser. She had laid well over a thousand eggs in her time and had hatched a hundred goslings. She was not a Christmas goose, never! She had learned the secret of peace, she was capable of a perpetual, graceful movement about the yard, a slow circling like an accomplished dervish, she moved with enviable regularity through her days and weeks and years, through her mating, laying and hatching. Reynolds followed the long feathers of her tail, his head low against the ground, following, following. The sphincter! What a muscle! What a dark well, the closed door to the mysteries of creation! Like a mouth, opening slowly to utter the Word, EGG! Closing again on its privacy. Fragrant, soft, and powerful.

Reynolds shifted gently on his chair. As he did so, three young boys from Heatherfield Close came walking precariously along the narrow wall-top behind the houses of the Park. They wanted to see if they could get the whole way round the Park, while simply walking on the wall. Here, at the Reynolds place, it seemed easier; there was the chicken wire to hold on to, and then there were the branches of the sycamore tree reaching out over the wall into the Keyhole.

The three boys paused. They could see Reynolds asleep on the chair beneath them. The yard was still, though filled with a rich quietness, of feeding, and scrabbling, and brooding. Nearer the back door of the house was the apple tree, a tree as old as the neighbourhood, already laden down with fruit. The boys knew that Reynolds would let the apples fall one by one onto the ground beneath the tree; the apples would lie there until they were fretted and pecked into nothing by the feeding fowl. The apples were still green, but plumping well. It would be a good time ...

Ducks, Reynolds was dreaming, the wiggling tail of a waddling duck! What a beauty, what grace and finesse in that wiggle. And when they up-arsed themselves in the pond and their webbed feet worked smoothly to keep that extraordinary balance, that cock-of-the-snook to the whole damn world, what freedom, what maturity, what confidence! The egg of the Aylesbury Duck is especially rich when she has fed on windfall apples. With the Pekin and The Duclair, the Rouen duck, like the front row of a scrum, hefty, bottom-waggers, head-down and go-for-it ducks. Reynolds's ducks were all fat and fair, being well fed on liver and cows' paunches, as well as rice, Indian meal, boiled potatoes, and pollard. They were dozing, now, under the shadow of a fuchsia hedge, their heads tucked in to their abundant feathers, their little eyes glazed and sleepy.

In under the apple tree, in the shade of the sycamore, several grey lag geese were busy; there were Emden geese as well, and some Poland and Chinese geese. A whole scatter of goslings, never having known the dangers of the world, were indulging their youth in the glow of the sunshine, their mothers barely conscious of them.

When Karl O'Brien, nine years of age, dropped from the lowest branch of the sycamore tree into the yard, he was as sudden and as terrible as a diving hawk. Still high in the branches of the tree were Kevin Dunter and Junior Sam O'Hare, the first a mere eight years of age, the latter almost twelve. At once the mother geese raised their heads and hissed; then, in a body, they charged, screeching, hissing, rushing, the whole of Reynolds's yard came alive with feathers and screaming and bodies flying hither and yon with overwhelming alacrity. Reynolds woke to a certain Armageddon.

All about him his fowl were scattering and shouting, ducks, geese, hens, there was much shaking of the branches of the sycamore tree. Hawks! Or those murdering, scavenging magpies! Reynolds reached quickly for his shotgun, brought it out into the sunlight, raised it towards the top of the tree and blasted!

UPSTAIRS

'Please, please stay, just this one evening, you could miss out on this one evening,' she pleaded with him, 'please, Jimmy, for my sake.'

It was too much to ask, she knew, but she was frightened, really frightened. When she saw the tears fill up his eyes she hugged him to her, tears scrabbling somewhere behind her own eyes as she whispered over his head,

'It's OK, it's OK, it's OK. You must go. Don't mind me at all. I'm just an old woman, old and stupid now the sun is going down.'

Immediately he found a small source of generosity, drawing back from her, looking up into her face, asking,

'Are you sure, Nanna? cos I really would stay if you really wanted me to.'

She was looking far beyond him now, her eyes narrowed, but she smiled and said,

'You must promise me, though, you must promise me not to say anything to anybody about what I asked you. Don't tell them I asked you. Promise? Will you promise me that?'

'Of course,' he said, deeply relieved, 'I promise, Nanna, I promise.'

Then he was gone.

She heard him open and shut the back door, heard the revving of the car, the sound of the wheels over the gravel. The silence settled back about her, the objects, the furniture standing in a tangible fug of stillness, familiar and unfamiliar at the same time. She shuddered and moved quickly to check if he had somehow locked the back door behind him. He hadn't. She was glad. She put on the light in the back kitchen; it shone dimly, a soft, watery eye in the evening brightness; she was not comforted.

Back through the kitchen and out into the front porch. Her slippers made an ugly, slitherful sound on the stone flags. It was bright here, too, a dull green and red shape on the floor from the coloured, frosted glass on the front door. A ghost, shifty, mould-and-blood-coloured. She opened the door and stood a short while on the threshold, looking out over the garden, the nearer fields, then the hotch-potch plotting and piecing of field and hedgerow as far as the sea. Nobody moved on the road, in the fields, on the water. The tide would be slopping away about the pier, great ugly jellyfish with their long, slithery feelers trailing through the water. Evil spirits; stings in their tails. Pallid. Silent. Alive with what could not be called life.

'It's all in your head,' they would tell her, 'it's all going on only in your head.'

She shivered and closed the door, making sure it was unlocked. She switched on the light in the hallway. The green and red ghost prostrate on the floor vanished at once.

She went back into the kitchen and took up her usual place by the open fire. Perhaps, now, she should pray. There was a certain comfort from the sound of the fire, a common-sense, normal shifting and settling. She sat back on the fireside chair and blessed herself. God himself, out of his great age, would have sympathy and understanding for her at this stage of her journey; he would forgive her for not kneeling down. She had long ago forgiven him his trespasses. She looked up at the tiny pink cross in the light before the statue; a steady, un-quenchable light. A comfort.

She began to say the words, mouthing them so that she could feel the shape and weight of them, bubbles moving and escaping into the world. So that they sounded first in her own head, knocking under her palate and spreading like an echo upwards, through the brain. The ticking of consonants, the shushing of vowels. Sounds that would drown out any other sounds she might not wish to hear. She moved her heavy body on the fireside chair and the springs and old timbers creaked a little, like her bones. Comforting, too, familiar, nameable sounds. 'The First Mystery ... '

Gradually her lips closed over the sounds she was making though they went on tipping and tapping on the roof of her mouth. She turned the small green-glass beads between her fingers, following the path of the rosary round which she had wandered daily for some seventy-five years. Round and round and round. On the very rim, now, of the great wheel of living, where God himself sat, weary, waiting. She held them up to the flickering light from the fire, seeing how the brightness made tiny, shimmering sea-caves against her skin.

A door slammed shut upstairs and she sat up, terrified. Now her mouth opened wide but no sound came out; her whole body began to tremble. Oh how she wished he had agreed to stay with her! She would have sent him upstairs to check if there was a window open somewhere in the back rooms, that would have caused a draught, that would have slammed shut the door.

'Here Jimmy,' she would have said, 'here's a half-crown for you; only don't tell your parents, buy whatever you like, bulls' eyes, cough lozenges, liquorice ... '

'A draught, that's all Nanna, only a draught ... '

She listened, straining one side of her body towards the door. There was no other sound. She was certain there was someone upstairs, or some *thing*, some awful, forbidden, unmentionable, *thing*. She held her breath a long time, lest it hear her breathing. 'The Second Mystery ... ' She forced herself on with the prayers, sounding them very deep down inside herself where only God could hear and understand.

'In your own head, Nanna, that's all,' they would have assured her. 'There is no place safer in the whole world than right here,' they would tell her, 'no robbers, no killers, no lunatics,' and she was older than any of them, and wiser, and she knew there was no such thing as ghosts? Of course, of course, she knew that, she would say, but ... Yes, she would say, yes, but still ...

A turf shifted easily in the fire and she smiled with confidence as she named the sound to herself. Had she ever seen a ghost? No! But still ... there was the time ... She stopped herself again. 'The Third Mystery ... '

By now they would be settled in their seats, munching crisps or chocolate or pop-corn. There would be a dull and muffled throb of conversation, clacking of seats up or down, a faint music talking at them from the walls. And soon the lights would begin to dim, there would be a hush, general, expectant, and the big curtains would begin to draw back, of themselves, to reveal the matt snow-covered field of the screen. They would not be thinking of her at all, now, not at all, not remotely.

There had been that time she was standing in this very kitchen, around noon, and the revolving earth came to a stop. She was young then, newly married, taking long pauses out of the circles of her days to hold herself up to a new awareness, of her body, her love, the breathless fear and expectancy with which she thought of herself, and of him. She would stand there, at the ironing table, a fresh scent rising from the damp clothes, the sheets, his shirts, his linens, and feel her breasts swelling proud and powerful, the strange cataclysmic uncoiling of something far away within her. She would twist and twist at the ring newly placed on her finger and smile out at the silence about her, knowing that silence was smiling back. Then, that day, as she stood, simply existing, two hot coals trapped in the heavy iron, waiting to make the linens breathe aloud, it had happened.

As if something had suddenly shifted, slipped in the mechanisms of time and she glimpsed, through the big window, four young men she did not recognise, or did she? dressed in dark suits of a strange cut, walking, in utter silence, over the gravel, carrying on their shoulders a coffin, its brass fittings glowing in the sunlight, the polish of the wood displaying a perfection beyond perfection, and as they passed, so incredibly slowly, just there beyond her, the coffin lid had lifted and a face she thought was familiar, yet that she could not place, gazed straight in at her for a moment; an old woman's face, very white, wholly expressionless. And that was all. Had she blinked then? because suddenly there was nothing, not even an absence of something that might have been. Only a catch in her throat that she thought would choke her, a trembling in her whole body, a chill that took every inch of her flesh instantly and left her shocked, dizzy, in mortal terror.

She had knocked against the ironing table in her hurry and had rushed out into the garden, to Ted, who had held her, and coaxed her, and walked her back into the house, his arms about her,

'It's your imagination, love, that's all, something that happened only inside your head,' the old-garden smell of his sweat reassuring her. One of the coals had fallen through the little trap-door in the back of the iron and had burned a hole through one of their wedding-sheets,

'Look,' he had said, laughing, 'the exact shape of a loving heart,' and she had laughed, too, and together they had walked about the house, seen the undisturbed gravel driveway, the closed gate, the empty road.

Now, she got up. Glory be to the Father, and to the Son and to the Holy Ghost ... and went over to draw the curtains on that very window. Then she switched on the light in the kitchen and drew the curtains on the window facing the road. Poor Ted, she thought, a good, good man, God rest his soul.

She heard footsteps move slowly across her own bedroom floor upstairs. She sat down again, petrified, as the dull, thudding sound echoed softly through the stone and timber of the old house. Three steps, perhaps four, that was all. Then nothing. Silence. Electrified. Her whole body buzzing with the thrum of her fear, her two hands gripping the arms of the chair, the small glass beads cutting into the palm of her hand. They would laugh at her, of course, should she tell them. Only the water in the cistern, they'd say, or the walls or the floors contracting or expanding before the cool of the evening. They'd laugh gently at her fears, at their own certainty.

'The Fourth Mystery ... ' She tried to settle down again but all her senses were alert to the upstairs. There was one sound that came, like a distant thud, like a chair moved on the carpet upstairs. She waited to hear footsteps again, and what she dreaded with a fear that made her almost ill — a door opening, footsteps descending the stairs. She found herself pleading with Ted, please Ted, please help me, pray for me, Ted, pray for me.

Then she screamed. There was a sudden, imperative knocking on the floor of her bedroom. Upstairs. Short. Loud. Three firm taps. She had chilled all over, as she had done so many years before. Rigid. Then there was silence. No sound at all. But she was certain. And her certainty gave her a degree of calmness she was grateful for. If she heard the door, and footsteps moving down the stairs, she knew now she would be able to escape quickly, out the back door, across the yard, out the gate, down the road to the comfort of Mrs Claine's old red house.

'The Final Mystery ... ' Our Father. She stopped. By now the cartoons would be over, perhaps the trailers for future attractions. There would be the ads., then lights up and curtains closed for a while to allow the people buy their packets of sweets, their drinks, their tubs of ice cream. There would be such a long time to wait and suffer yet before they came home, the faint light on the curtains outside, strengthening, the sound of the car turning in and slowing along the gravel, the doors opening, the sound of voices ... It was no good. She could not go on like this. She would simply have to face it out.

Surprised at her own calmness and determination she stood up and straightened the clothes about her old, tired body. She gripped the beads tightly in her hand and began to move from the warm kitchen. How all her bones ached; how the weariness of living seemed to concentrate about her ankles and move slowly up her legs, as if the spinning of the great cart-wheel of life were slowing to a stop. She would have the banisters to hold on to, she would face it now at last, climb the stairs herself, what was there left to lose?

When the lights came up in the cinema his father was surprised that young Jimmy didn't rush to the usherette for his bag of liquorice allsorts. He just sat there, abstracted, his mouth closed but working, his young brow puckered. He moved close up to his father and held his right arm, looking up into his eyes.

'I'm worried about Nanna,' he whispered, 'you know, I don't think she's well. And she's frightened. She was begging me to stay with her tonight and not come to the pictures. And now I've told you, and she made me promise not to tell. A broken promise is a fallen star and a fallen star is a soul loosed out of life. That's what Nanna always used to say ... '

THE JUNIPER FILES

'Not worth a balloon,' the old man had said as he pointed out their mooring spot in the harbour. 'Not worth a balloon, out there in that oul' punt beside them yachts, hey? Hah?' and he had laughed loudly, wiping a salty drop from his nose.

They were well out to sea by now, past Ireland's Eye, a mile or so from the harbour. Lambay Island their destination but already this was a hopeless dream. The afternoon had grown dark and brooding, a nasty wind — threatening before noon — now beginning to make itself felt.

'White horses,' the old man had said, 'there's white horses a-galloping out there beyond the harbour mouth, shouldn't gerout in a punt like that... Not me, lads, not youz either, if youz have any sense at all.'

Now even Diamond was looking anxious. There was a sudden scuffle of wind and a small spittle of spray went over them. Lambay became a grey sore on the back of their brains.

'Maybe we'll turn back,' Diamond muttered, 'take on the whole thing some other day when we've more time and the weather is a little easier.'

Juniper agreed at once; he had been nervous, though resolute, from the start. Diamond began to turn the boat about. The 'Double D', fourteen feet, clinker built, sanded down, three coats of the best marine varnish. But a craft for the mighty main? Not worth a balloon, lads, not worth a balloon.

Diamond, in the stern, held the tiller with a certain

grimness. Slevin, huddled into his wind-cheater, huddled into himself, no lover of the sea, in the bows.

The boat began to come round, bucking, tossed now by the running sea. Port side on a wave struck, she lurched, heeled, and settled. The spray had drenched them at one go.

'Jesus, we'll be drowned,' Slevin screeched.

'Juniper!' hissed Diamond, 'get the oars and start rowing; we've just got to get the boat round.'

Juniper began pulling hard on one oar. The boat came about, chin up, facing at last back towards Howth, now a dark blotch on the horizon with a few lights already lit along the hillside. Juniper's back was towards the land and he was watching Diamond's face; Diamond was worried, that strained look on his well-tanned face, that ferocity in his grip on the tiller, eyes scanning the coming waves.

'Come on, Slevin, row!' he shouted.

Slevin, geography man, landlubber, earth-lover, scared motionless, clutching the gunwales. But he jerked into action at Diamond's order and took up another pair of oars.

'Queen of Heaven have mercy on us!' he called out.

Straight on now, into tide and wind, head on, backs into it.

'Row, lads, for Christ's sake row.'

Juniper glanced around; Slevin was pulling on the oars, clumsily; darkness, the great dun chest of a horse, looming; the seas coming, beautiful, dark green, and white. Not much headway being made, if any; then a bigger wave; they rose. And dropped. The outboard engine coughed, stopped. At once they could feel the sea take them in its power, the boat a leaf in a storm-full drain, Diamond tugging frantically at the starter; it caught again, and sang.

'We'll have to ease her a bit to starboard, lads,' Diamond shouted. 'Just row as hard as you can, I'll keep moving her a little to the right. If we get in behind Ireland's Eye there'll be less wind, we can get round it and head in to the harbour from the other side.'

The boat juddered again, rebelled, then yielded. They could make it, perhaps. Perhaps. With a sense of relief Juniper shouted:

'And I haven't even begun to found my city yet!'

'To Hell with your city, Dukes, just row!'

Juniper rowed. His arms were stiff, his breathing difficult, the backs of his legs strained. He kept his thoughts off it; welkin — the welter; driving the sea-flocks before us. Speak to the mariners. The salt sea spray. Life itself, precarious, so easily snuffed out. Not worth a balloon, lads, not worth a balloon.

'Heigh my hearts,' Juniper sang, 'tend to the master's whistle.'

No response; Slevin's face was a resentful mask, and Diamond's set hard with determination. They were going to make it, crabbing into the shelter of the island, outboard and oars moving them noticeably closer to the rocks and the cliffs of Ireland's Eye.

'Play the men, now, play the men,' Juniper screamed, with more relief in his voice than he yet wished to allow himself. They could hear, above the sound of the wind, the yikkity-yikkity-yak of the kittiwakes about the rocks, and once a puffin flew low and near. Then the wind was cut off and they were able to ease the boat gently round the island and into the comparative calm of the bay.

Slevin began to discover a vein of joy and banter; they were able to stop rowing and the engine took them along the coast and in among the larger yachts in the harbour.

'Well, Dukes,' Slevin mocked, 'we're not for the drowning this time. Must be destined for the hanging later on. Well, ye can keep yer oul' boat to yerselves; ye won't catch me coming out in it again.'

At last they were scrambling up the iron ladder onto the quay. As Juniper's head came level with the wet quayside he bent forward and kissed it; '*habemus papum*', he announced gravely.

'*Papam*, you eejit, Dukes, *papam*,' Diamond said.

'The lovely, feminine Pope,' Slevin laughed, and they were on dry land. Drenched, they changed from their wind-cheaters in the car, shaking the sea from them, scraping death off the yellow brilliance of the plastics, rolling them up with relief.

'Right, lads,' Diamond announced, 'hot whiskeys are called for.' They made their way towards a pub further down the town, brightly lit, in the deepening gloom of the August evening; 'The Bull's Mouth', welcoming and dry after their ordeal. Out of the maw of the ocean and into the mouth of the bull.

* * *

It was like entering a red cave, plum-red lighting everywhere, red wallpaper, red plush seats and red-topped tables; the overall impression was of luxury, a well-wrought city over beyond the edges of a struggling world. They sat together in a corner, relaxing quickly over the whiskeys.

Diamond chewed on a clove. Latin master. He said:

'Do you know, we've risked the mad bitch Scylla and we've risked the cliffs and we've made it through.'

Juniper began to warm from within. But he swore, in his mind, that one day soon he would have a bigger boat, better in every way, not with mast and sails, too much labour in all of that, but a cabin cruiser whose bows would rise gallantly out of the waters and take such a wind and sea as they had known today totally in its stride.

He noticed three attractive young women sitting on bar stools, up against the bar; they were chatting together. He watched them, as he allowed the liquor to seep its potency into his imagination; there he was, under a rich blue sky, his

cruiser gliding effortlessly on the waves, under cliffs somewhere off the southern coast of France, Juniper standing tall
at the helm, and on the deck before him these beautiful
women, stretched out to the sun, topless, the cabin waiting,
a well-stocked bar, adequate sleeping accommodation. James
A. Dukes, high-flyer, captain, killer, suave; buccaneer, wind-
surfer, life-surfer, king ... some day, some day; but it had
better be soon!

It came to Juniper's turn to buy a round. He went to the
bar and stood close beside the women. As he waited for the
barman to boil the kettle, he was caressing each full, firm
body in turn, his hands moving gently all over them, his body
fitting snugly against theirs. Once he glanced at one of them
and she was watching him, as if she knew, as if she could
sense the ocean churning inside his brain; the contact was
brief and distant but Juniper blushed and turned away, disturbed. Where could he find comfort? She was so lovely,
bright of face, eager and young. And his loneliness hurt him,
as if someone had punched him, hard, and he could double
up with the pain of it. The lounge was a mist-filled fen where
spirits moved about, randomly, alone, without sound, each
spirit real, each an illusion. No contact possible, no contact
allowed. Why can we not join, hand to hand, body to body,
and be together? Always this strife inside, this perpetual and
numbing pain.

The longing that he had was for sexual contact, too, full
and passionate, to explore and taste and know every pore
and orifice and angle of a woman's body and to come from
the contact with all his senses exhausted and satisfied; and
more — much more — to know that this was but one way of
melting his own life into that of another so that the isolation,
the loneliness, the empty morass of living could be overcome.
Tears in the very nature of things, the heart pained by tran-
sience, lives apart yet urgent towards one another, silenced
souls passing in the fog, like individual ketch, canoe or

coracle that may touch, collide, and draw away quickly into isolation.

The barman was offering him his change, the whiskeys steaming in front of him; he started out of his pain and took the coins. As he put them into his trouser pocket and began to gather up the glasses, he could feel the cold smallness and indifference of the coins as they began to slip through a hole in his pocket, race down his leg and fall with a ringing insistence on the marble floor of the lounge. As he reached to pick them up all the misery of life seemed to throng together behind his eyes; he was wet again and cold, there was a gale blowing in his face, the boat would, of course, make it through the tempest but only after hours of effort and despair, would make it back to an empty quay, the long slithering arms of seaweed reaching out to him and the rusted steps of the quay wall the only cold contact he would have with the earth. He looked up at the three women but they were talking together, unaware of his confusion, the sudden lethargy in his movements, the deep crimson of his face. Not worth a balloon, lads, not worth a balloon.

† † †

It was raining as the Dukes family drove through Newport and took the turn under the old railway bridge towards Castlebar. Croagh Patrick should have been visible but it had disappeared under the rain. All about them the fens and bogs were dark and the winds raced and contended through fern and heather, up and down the turf banks, in and out of the black pools. Once the wipers gave way and they had to travel at a snail's pace until they reached a garage outside Longford. Here they waited for an hour before the problem was rectified and still the rains poured down and the winds lashed the car; there were floods on the roads, the insides of the windows were steamed up. They lost their way twice among the windings of the suburbs until at last — as if they had finally moored a craft against a quay wall — they turned in through an old, grey archway and were driving up a tree-shaded avenue that led to the great door of a manor.

Mr Dukes got out of the car and ran to the door, James and his mother and Nora, his grandmother, waiting, watched anxiously through the rain. The massive door was quickly opened and Mr Dukes was drawn inside. Almost at once he was beckoning from the half-open door; James helped his grandmother, holding the umbrella over her; Mrs Dukes ran awkwardly on her high heels over the wet gravel; Grandmother, slow and shaken, her footsteps heavy, almost unwilling, almost lost. James returned to the car and brought his big, black suitcase.

'Welcome, welcome, welcome!'

It was a large, red-faced and jovial-looking monk that received them. He clanged the heavy door to behind them and shook hands with the adults. Then he clapped James on the back.

'Well, well, well! James, isn't it? Welcome, lad, welcome. What a terrible day! I'm sure you'd all like a nice, hot cup of tea?'

He led them down a brown corridor. There were plaster statues of saints standing on narrow plinths, ranged at regular intervals along the sides of the corridor. The damp shoes of the visitors made a sighing sound on the brown linoleum. Through another big door, along another narrow, smaller corridor of a vaguely blue shade with frosted, arched windows on one side and a series of green-baize-covered doors on the other. James heaved his suitcase along, pausing to shift the weight from one hand to the other.

The monk opened a door at the end of this corridor and ushered them into a large conservatory, high and rounded, the glass ceiling with slender filaments of green iron running across it. There was an overwhelming scent of geraniums. For the dead. For the living. There were exotic plants, high palm trees, lilies, orchids. In the guarded atmosphere James felt numbed, as if he had been hauled half-alive from the sea and left on a foreign strand.

There were several standing round, young men of about his own age, with their parents. There was half-hearted chat, a sense of constraint and tension. The adults had cups of tea which they held away from them, as if scared of them; young eager monks were moving about with enamel teapots and fragile plates of biscuits and buns.

Mr and Mrs Dukes were talking to a tall, gaunt brother. James watched his grandmother; she was seated on a garden chair at the end of the conservatory, sipping her tea, looking lost. She was large-boned, dressed in black, her thin hair held in a light-brown net; he knew the awkward, big bras and corsets she wore, the number of cardigans she needed to keep out the cold; she was what he knew best of the past, her struggles with the great events of history, her memories of death and loneliness, her eyes now beginning to focus on her own death. He moved over to her. She stood up slowly and drew him to her, held him tightly, and he felt her body heave with the sobs.

'I'm sorry to be such a softie, James, such a softie, but I know I won't live to see you ordained. Father James. Father James Dukes. I'm so very, very proud of you!'

He knew the thick scent of her talcum, the tears were smudging the powders on her old face. Nanna.

Then his parents were saying goodbye; suddenly they were gone, back out the same door through which they had entered, led out by the same loud, monk. James watched them go; there was one awful moment when he was going to call out after them, call to say it was all a great mistake. Take me home, take me back to what I know, the island, the sea, the moors. But they had gone. He stood, holding an empty cup; in the moist heat of the conservatory the tall lilies seemed

to droop and wilt. He felt washed out, dispirited. On the floor
beside him was the future, a suitcase filled with the trim and
tackle of a new life.

* * *

Juniper lived alone in a semi-detached house close to the
estuary of Malahide; three beds, a lounge-cum-kitchen-cum-
diningroom, a bathroom, a downstairs toilet and washhand
basin, a garage and a small garden front and rear. Modest.
The reward for following along the pathway of truth.

He came home from 'The Bull's Mouth' a little off the
upright. Just a few days before he had bought a simple gas
fire and had lugged it upstairs into the fortress of his 'study'
(one of the three bedrooms) where he went at times to try and
put a few lines of poetry together. Now he lit the fire and went
downstairs for something — he could not remember what —
and then came back upstairs. The study was ablaze; the coat,
on a chair, the sleeve, the papers, the curtains — all in a matter
of minutes, or was it seconds?

He rushed downstairs for a bucket of water. He found no
bucket. He came back upstairs. The room was alive with the
noise of the fire; it seemed that a great roaring laughter came
from every part of the house. He stood and watched it from
the top of the landing, numbed again with the old sense of
frustration. Why me? why me again? He dived for the phone.
Why me?

There's the name, for a start: James Dukes. James Bleedin'
Dukes! Strange how different initial letters produce the same
initial, cluttered sound: jay, dew, j, Jew, although of course
there are some who would pronounce it Dyukes, or Deeuks,
and Jewx. Heh! A harsh-sounding name, crass and brassy,
two sounds allied yet different, unmusical, unpoetic. I am
mongrel dog and mongrel cat, I am meaningless, God's fool.

Friends and neighbours called him Jimmy; *Jimmy Dukes,*

more musical, more friendly, more familiar, *Jimmy Dukes*, softer, more full of caresses, more sexy... Which brought to mind Marie-Claire next door, the French woman married to the bus-driver, Brendan Flynn, the Flynns, and their house in this agglomeration of the unrich and the unhopeful.

Their bedroom was just beyond the wall next to Juniper's bedroom and on quiet nights he could hear them in action in there, and he curled down under the bedclothes to keep himself from screaming. He knew their room was painted all over in navy blue, floor and walls and ceiling, curtains too of unpatterned blue, the carpet a rich, deep blue, like the sea. He knew that the bed they had was a water-bed and they went to sea together on it, riding the waves together, splashing, sinking, surfacing, sending ripples of despair through the wall into Juniper's dry soul. He was certain they were at sea when he rang their doorbell long and urgently and Brendan came down in a dressing-gown — hers, of course — to find out what was the matter. Before he had opened his door, however, the sound of the fire-engine was audible on the main road; a glance gave Brendan full knowledge of what was going on. He shouted back up the stairs:

'Marie-Claire, quickly, Jimmy's house is on fire!'

Juniper could see Marie-Claire coming down the stairs in a flimsy, light-blue nightdress. For a moment, with the landing light behind her, the shape of her body was shadowed through to Jimmy's eyes. A mermaid on a rock, lusted after, then diving away into the depths. Oh she was lovely, lovely, lovely!

'Poor Cheemy,' she cooed, 'poor, poor Cheemy, what is happening?'

That name, in her mouth! when the J became as soft as her own French tongue, warm and moist as ... and when the i became more of an eee, and she seemed to linger on the name: Cheemy, Cheeeeemy, Cheeeeeeeee-my... oh my God what she could do to him if only... if only...

Everywhere the world was scarlet with noise; men were
clearing people out of the houses on either side of Juniper's
— Brendan and Marie-Claire and their little daughter Nicole,
the tiny dog 'Chien' who was barking his stupid head off and
being held close by the angel in her almost transparent
nightie — the neighbours on the other side to whom he had
scarcely ever spoken. They watched as a hose was rushed
through the hall door and up the stairs, and then the whole
water system of suburbia was turned onto Juniper's study.

Soon, the danger past, Marie-Claire threw the dog from
her and gripped Juniper by the arm.

'Poor, poor Cheeemy, oh what can we do to help?'

Juniper imagined there was a little more in it than pity, but
then he had had a few too many....

'Brendan!' she went on, 'Cheemy must stay the rest of this
night with us. We have the extra bed in the front room. You
must sleep with us during this night, Cheemy.'

Oh God, oh Holy God! Soon Juniper found himself nestling down on a very comfortable bed, against a slim partition
that separated this room from that of Marie-Claire. He did
not sleep well; he sailed a rough sea, alien, ailing, alone. The
study was a blackened hulk; this thing of darkness he would
have to acknowledge as his own. *And what seest thou else in
the dark backward abysm of time?* — only Marie-Claire, a few
feet from him, the water-bed in motion and Brendan afloat
on ecstacy, nobody to grind her lovely body against the sweet
and willing flesh of Jimmy Dukes. Was he too old now ever
to find love? Had he missed out on life? skulking elsewhere
while the fresh and sap-filled years were slipping by? Hell
was empty that night and all the devils were in Juniper's
head.

About five o'clock in the morning Juniper decided to take
firm steps. James A. Dukes to take the stage. By now he had
a few poems published here and there under that name, a
literary name, a slow name, with dignity to it, the A with its

period giving a rhythmic balance to the sounds and leaving a certain something of mystery hovering by. Somewhere down the road he would find himself, find confidence, assertiveness and may, he thought to himself, may the angel go with me on the road.

* * *

After the fire, after the tortured night next bed to Marie-Claire, Juniper had determined to start afresh on foreign soil. It was August; he would make one more attempt to find love in this city and then, should that fail, he would ... Soon the dreadful maritime-suburban winter would set in, the long, painful term from January to April would follow with its rains, frosts and slushes, cars refusing to start, the hideous warts and wens of the pupils in steamy classrooms day upon day upon day ... How can the human soul thrive? 'Freedom, high day! High day, freedom!'

He met Diamond and Slevin once again in a corner of 'The Bull's Mouth'.

'But what kind of a boat will it be?' Slevin asked.

'Well,' Juniper began, 'a couple of doors down from me there's this house with a fine boat perpetually moored on the lawn. They're aspiring yuppies, the boat is for show. It hasn't shifted from the lawn during the two years I've been in the Court. I've spoken to the chap and he's very willing to sell. They're about ready to buy a bigger house somewhere else and he's keen to get the cash.'

'How much?'

'Just two grand.'

'Yes, but what kind of a boat is it?'

'It's twenty feet, a cabin cruiser, inboard engine, forty horse power, I think. Two berths. It's not in perfect shape but I'll bring it up to my place and I can work on it over the winter and spring, do it up, make it cosy, put in as much equipment and stuff as I'll need.'

'Make it all tight and yare, like,' offered Diamond.

'There's a fine cabin I can make perfectly comfortable, a home even. I'll get the house sold around March, pay off the mortgage; that'll leave me with about twenty thousand clear, keep me going for a while. Then there'll be money from the job, I don't know how much yet, but it'll be a few grand at least. I can spend the months of May and June maybe off the coast of Ireland, getting used to handling her, getting to know the sea, how to read charts or maps or whatever. I'll always stay close to the shore. Then at some stage, when I'm ready, I'll just head off, over to Wales on the best day I can find, round the coast, over to France, down the coast of France, Spain, Portugal, into the Mediterranean. Then I'll cross over to Italy, put in somewhere south of Naples and winter there. I'll not spend too much money, stay close to the coast, ready to put in if the weather is even a little bit hairy. Then I'll get a job in a town in Italy, teaching English, live in the boat until I find a small place of my own. A fishing village in the south of Italy, from where I can cruise. The Greek Islands. The coast of Africa. Egypt, anywhere!'

'Now the topless towers have burned down,' the Latin master said, 'you're off to Italy to found your Rome. I suppose we'll have to call it a Duke-dom.'

'It's a totally daft scheme,' the landlubber, the ground-hugger, Slevin, interrupted; 'no future, no security. God I think you're nuts to throw up a well-paid job and head off into the darkness.'

'Not the darkness, the light.'

'You have one hell of an imagination,' Slevin finished.

'By keeping the coastline within reach, having on board even the minimum safety equipment, say an inflatable dinghy, where's the risk? Move only when the elements are with me, gather unto myself treasure on earth, sunlight, freedom. Think of the adventure, the possibilities, the sunflowers, the vines, old towns guarding themselves on the tops of hills, warm, brown, rich in love and history. Like the swallows I'll be where the sunlight is. And you lot! you'll be standing in your classrooms with Brother Canice hovering outside the door, rain pouring down the windows and the bad breath of the lads clogging the insides of your brains and they'll all be sitting there in front of you, sneering. Freckled whelps, hag-born, the lot of them!'

† † †

Brother Jerome McCarthy spent the afternoon practising the piano in a small, musty room at the top of the house. Brother Jerome was short, stumpy and very round; it was a perpetual wonder to the Brothers how Jerome ever managed to get his feet to reach the pedals of the great organ in the Chapel. When he played voluntaries as the monks processed out of their stalls, Brother Jerome was to be seen in frantic motion, his chubby fingers and his chubby feet moving at an enormous rate, his chubby backside sliding all over the well-polished organ seat.

Brother Jerome was intent on trekking, with distinction, down the arduous path towards perfection staked out centuries before by the Founder. The only *divertissement* along the way could be the playing of secular pieces on the piano. On this particular afternoon he was working on Mozart's '*Rondo a la Turca*'. For two hours and more he stitched and un-stitched, picked, pecked and pocked at '*Rondo a la Turca*'. His playing, while it gave no great evidence of musical skills, proved at least that if dedication, persistence, and hope could make a man into a saint, these virtues might also be applied to the learning of Mozart's '*Rondo a la Turca*'.

Brother James Dukes happened to be in a room close to the piano room. His task was to study the life of the Venerable Founder and prepare a detailed paper on the theme of

'Leprosy and the Will of God as exhibited and developed in the events of the life of, and articulated in the writings of, the Venerable Founder'. It was a dusky, sleepy afternoon, good for the soul, however much the head might nod, or the words of the Venerable Founder blur across the page.

Later that evening all the Brothers knelt in silent meditation in the Chapel. The little red light in the sanctuary stirred and shifted. The Holy Ghost floated high above the bowed heads. Brother James Dukes, attempting to meditate on the theme of 'leprosy of the soul', found his brain swollen tight with the memory of *Rondo a la Turca*. His eyes were closed, his head lowered gravely over his folded hands, but in the secret centre of his head all that surfaced was Mozart's *Rondo a la Turca*. Ta ti ta ti tum, ta ti ta ti tum, ta ti ta ti ta ti ta ti ta ti ta ti tum, tum tum la ta pa ta, la ta pa ta, la ta pa ta pum... over and over and over and over and over again. He opened his eyes for a moment and glanced about, fearing the others might be listening to what was going on in his head.

All the Brothers seemed deeply immersed in their own, sacred, wildernesses. Brother Jerome McCarthy knelt bolt upright, his eyes closed, a sheen on his large forehead. Brother Marcel Piat, eyes closed, too, was wiping his nose with an immaculate handkerchief. Brother Luke O'Mahony was swaying gently to either side in an ecstasy of prayer. Brother James bowed his head once more, recited a few established prayers, called upon the Founder; ta ti ta ti tum, ta ti ta ti tum...

He opened his eyes again and gazed up at the Altar in a plea for aid; there was the tiny, scarlet flame in the sanctuary lamp announcing the presence amongst them of the Risen Lord himself, images of his Sacred Heart, the fire of his love, the immolation of his body. The little tongue of flame was moving rhythmically, back and forth, back and forth, ta ti ta ti tum.....

Brother James shifted unhappily on his pew; the creak of

the timbers seemed to echo in the Chapel like a gunshot; all the bowed heads remained low; God was passing among his chosen ones, encouraging, suggesting, cajoling, no doubt frowning with frustration on those unmoored. Brother Leo McGarvey, however, did appear to have his head bowed a little beyond the ordinary; his head lolled over the joined fingers and the fingers appeared to be sliding slowly, slowly, slowly, off the handrest. Leo's head lurched as the hands slipped; he snorted, opened his eyes, and was back in the land of the watchful.

Brother James held himself stiffly upright and met the startled eyes of Brother Leo across the choir. Leo winked. James lowered his head at once, closed his eyes, allowed his mind to ramble along the cliffs of his island, watching kitti-wake and fulmar soar in splendour over rough seas, hearing the long, mesmerising breaking of waves across the beach; he saw his family, spread out on rugs on a summer day, his grandmother, wrapped in her black clothes, her arms folded, gazing away over the sea into her memories ... and James's heart swelled with grief and loss, tears came gently to his eyes, and he bowed his head fully over his trembling hands.

* * *

Mid-August, the summer holidays drawing to their dreaded close. Juniper decided on a week in London. He sat for a while on the steps around and below the statue of Eros in Piccadilly Square. He had a salad sandwich roll and he knew its consumption would not be an easy affair. All around him younger people in fascinating combinations of colours and clothes, the with-it people, chatted and smoked, drinking beer from cans or cider from large plastic bottles. They were of those who have found their way in life, or of those who do not care what their way may be; those at home in the world, at home among other people.

Juniper got the cellophane off the roll and bundled it up into a small knob in his hand. He could see no litter bin anywhere. The steps were littered anyway so he brought his hand near the ground, looked up suddenly at the signs on the top of the buildings nearby and let the little scut of cellophane slip from his hand onto the steps. Litter-lout. He began to eat.

The sun shone on central London. There was a bewildering whirlpool of traffic, cars, lorries, red buses and tourist coaches, millions of bustling, purposeful folk, motorbikes, bicycles, noise, noise, noise. Two policemen were sauntering round the steps, chatting together. They were small, Juniper thought, compared to the Irish garda, small and dapper. Suave. None of the 'hey there youze whatchathink youze are at?', less of the cudgel, more of the poignard; the 'excuse me, sir, would you mind stepping ...' sort. Looking at them Juniper decided he would prefer the cudgel; quietly he gathered back the knob of cellophane and pocketed it.

He would stay a while, waiting for the afternoon to tick away a little more, gathering courage and excitement at the thought of Soho. It was pleasant in the sun though he felt out of place; his casuals too casual, his shirt too new, his shoes too polished. The roll too big for his mouth. Salad cream and slips of lettuce were clinging to his fingers. He tried to surprise the roll by taking a sudden leap at the end of it, but a blob of tomato fell on his new, cream trousers. He flicked it off. There was a stain.

Finally it was time for James A. Dukes to offer his pounds sterling for the joy, at last, of feeding on a woman's body. He began his walk through Soho. The cinema fronts had their enormous posters of naked women, the sex shops had loud, pounding music coming from within half-open doors, coloured lights winked, encouraged and cajoled. Juniper's stomach churned. As he walked along Dean Street he was stopped by a very attractive woman. She murmured something to him from a doorway.

'Sorry? I didn't quite catch what you said.'

'Oh, you're Irish, I love the Irish. Lovely.'

'I'm glad, sure and doesn't everybody?'

'Everybody sure does, honey, everybody sure does.'

'Can I help you?'

'Of course you can, honey, of course you can. Just thirty quid now and I'll show you the time of your life.'

'Oh,' stuttered Juniper, as the sun came out from behind the clouds. 'You're a... I mean, I, I don't know, I mean I never...'

'All the better, honey, all the better.' She took his arm and ushered him quickly along Dean Street. 'Come on, honey, just walk beside me a little way, friendly like, it mustn't seem as if I'm picking you up or anything, you know?'

'Oh no. I mean, yes. I understand. That's all right.'

There was butter thickening in his stomach.

'So, you've never had sex then? Where have you been all your life? My oh my, where on earth have you been? Still now, isn't it nice. I so admire a man who has been able to keep himself pure. And isn't this your lucky day? Darling you'll see, I'll give you such an introduction, such a beautiful, overwhelming introduction, you'll bless the day you found me. I'm good, you know, and not bad-looking, come on then, tell me, what do you think?'

Juniper glanced nervously at her; she was indeed very pretty, a lot of make-up perhaps, a heavy scent; he had a feeling there was a good deal of talcum powder about. But very pretty, brunette, well built, lively.

'I think you're beautiful,' he blurted out.

'Thankyou, honey, thankyou. You and I will get along just fine. You have thirty quid, don't you? It's not much to ask for the favours I'm going to do you.'

'Oh yes, I have. It's not that, though, I mean, I never have... and I don't know anything at all about anything like that.'

'There now, who'd believe that? It's perfectly allright, honey, perfectly allright. But you're not going to go through life in that awful condition, now are you? And after me you'll certainly have something to think about. Now is the very best time to learn a trick or two. Time you got your feet under you, isn't it? We'll take it all very slowly, you'll learn. I know a thing or two myself, make up for your loss, you see?'

They turned aside, suddenly, into a tiny café. 'Just so I can settle myself and make a phone call,' she said. The café was cluttered with tables and chairs; steam hissed from a large boiler, and coffee pots were stewing at the end of the counter. On the wall were pictures of plates of sausages and chips, burgers, beans; a variety of sandwiches and cream buns and flies littered the counter and the glass case beneath.

'We'll just have a coffee, honey, and I'll use the phone and get the room set up for us.'

She spoke to the man behind the counter, a large gentleman, with an apron far from white. She spoke quietly and he glanced over at Juniper; the would-be sailor on the ocean of love stood, burning, just inside the door.

She came towards him, carrying two cups of coffee.

'Sit down here now, honey, we'll just have the coffee first.'

They sat at a small, round plastic table. She began to drink her coffee at once, without milk or sugar. Juniper began to unwrap a lump of sugar but found it immensely difficult, his hands trembling, a continual, whirling movement going on somewhere inside his head, a fever deep down inside his stomach. He dropped it into the coffee. He slopped the milk, his hands refusing to follow the directions his addled head was sending down to them.

'What's your name, then, honey?'

'Jimmy,' he replied quickly. 'Jimmy, ah, McHugh.'

'Jimmy, that's nice. My name is Annabelle. Now Willie there at the counter tells me his phone is out of action so I'll just nip around to this little hotel where I work; I have a room

I use but I'll have to get it set up and I'll have to give the man the money. I'll need that thirty quid now so I can put the money on the room for the afternoon. Can I have it now, honey?'

Juniper fumbled out some notes and handed her the thirty pounds.

'You just drink up your coffee here and I'll be back to you in a jif. Bye, hon.' She licked her index finger and rubbed it to the tip of his nose. Then she was gone.

Juniper thought the coffee tasted like warm lake-water. He tried to drink it, aware of the large man at the counter. He wondered if the man was shocked at what was going on; would he say anything ...? But the man stood absently drawing rings on the glass top of his counter with a dirty rag. Juniper sipped at the coffee and sat back, as nonchalantly as he could. He thrummed his fingers on the plastic tabletop. He took another sip and as he was putting the cup down the door opened. The cup lurched in his hand and half the coffee slurped out onto the table. A boy came in, dropped some newspapers on the counter, grunted at the man and went out without giving Juniper a glance. Willie came round the counter with his dirty rag and began to mop up the coffee.

'That'll be two quid, minimum order charge,' he said.

Juniper looked up at him, astonished, then began to fumble about in the inside pocket of his jacket. Eventually he found a five-pound note and handed it over. The man said 'Ta very much' and kept mopping up. He picked up the cups and saucers, went behind the counter and vanished through the beaded curtain leading into some cave behind the shop. There was a long, long silence.

Juniper sat, quite still, for another five minutes, hoping the man would come back with his change, hoping that what he really knew to be true may not, after all, be true. Gradually a feeling close to nausea began to rise through his body. He got up, quickly, determined to get away as soon as possible, back into the fresh air round Piccadilly Circus.

*   *   *

Brother Anselm sat next to Brother James for meals. So it was
ordained, so it was, by God's will, expressed and accepted.
'Misery acquaints a man with strange bedfellows.'

Father Superior said grace before breakfast and there followed a fine rasping of chairs as all the postulants and all the
Brothers sat down together at the table of the Lord. On this
particular morning one of the novices was doing the refectory
readings; there were two novices on penance, kneeling out
on the wooden floor, hands joined, eyes down; they would
go without breakfast for three mornings, having spoken
together for a moment during the Great Silence. Monks and
postulants and novices all kept their heads low, their eyes
prudently fixed on the table in front of them. Silence was the
rule, the needs of the body must always be sublimated, the
body's demands being of the smallest importance in the per-
fecting of the whole man.

The lector climbed into the refectory pulpit and Brother
Anselm's right elbow dug into Brother James's left side;
Anselm always ate with relish and a great many flourishes.
Anselm; how quickly Brother James had come to hate and
despise Brother Anselm, Brother in Christ; Anselm, what a
name to take and expect it to ring true with Carmody! Brother
Anselm Carmody, seventy years of age, guzzling and suck-
ing and slurping at his porridge as if he were a babe in arms.

The young novice was reading the martyrology of the day;
Brother James tried to give his attention to the long list of
names in Latin, saints, virgins, martyrs, to whom this day
belonged; he imagined the heavenly table at which these
saints were being feted, the fine foods they would have, the
enormous cakes, saints and virgins and martyrs poised for
the blowing out of candles. For all his efforts to follow the
names, Brother James had to admit that could as well be a
catalogue of flowers, of fish, or trees; *Onercus agrifolia, eugenia*

apiculata, prunus lusitanica, juniperus hibernica ...

Brother Anselm had finished spooning stirabout into his holy person and was occupied in trying to persuade a tiny, milky lump of porridge onto his index finger for transfer to his mouth; another, large, lump had fallen down the front of his habit; like a slug it would move, slowly, down to the bib on Anselm's lap, leaving a delicate, silvery trace behind it to merge with all the other tracks and stains that had gathered about that same old path. Brother James tried to keep his eyes in custody, but they were drawn to the progress of the slug.

The serving Brothers removed the empty bowls — then they brought the huge, enamel pots of tea and set them down; with the tea came plates of 'black and tans,' slices of hot black pudding fried, with plump juicy sausages still bristling from the fat. The dish went round, clockwise, and all the monks, with saintly nonchalance, took one, or two, or sometimes three sausages and three to four, and sometimes five, coins of pudding. There was plenty to go round and indeed the dish could go round again, for labouring monks need a substantial fuel of grease and fat to get them through their day.

Brother James was tempted to take more black pudding than he ought because, to his left, Brother Anselm had abandoned custody of the eyes and was waiting eagerly for his turn — he would pop, Brother James knew well, the puddings whole into his mouth and suck and shiver them about, now bulging out his right cheek, now his left, with the blood of the pig — like a brat in school whose mouth is filled with gobstoppers — until the pudding became a churned mass within; then he would take a mouthful of tea and send the whole thing shuddering down his gullet with, James was convinced, a good imitation of the sound of a toilet being flushed.

The lector had finished with the martyrology and had taken up where last night's reader had left off: 'Treasure in

Heaven', by Rev. John Kearney CSSp. The youthful voice, eager, innocent and alert with faith and trust, caught Brother James's attention now and again.

' ... *We are the living stones that in God's design are to build up the eternal temple, the heavenly Jerusalem. In this world we are being so prepared that we may be ready to fill the place God has made ready for us. The preparation involves our being shaped and hammered. The corners must be broken off, probably with many blows; we must be polished, and only then are we fit for our place in the heavenly city...'*

Now the serving brothers brought out into the refectory the dishes of fried bread, slices of stale white bread from yesterday's meals, now fried golden and black and crisp in the fat of the puddings and sausages. To put the energy of lard into those who have to sweat it out in the vineyard of the Lord. The problem for Brother James was Brother Anselm Carmody's false teeth. They formed a sort of dance with castanets on the slices of fried bread, greatly adding to the discomfiture of his sensitive neighbours.

' ... *the special duty allotted to us in religion occupies a long space of time, a great part of our day. It may be of considerable interest and considerable difficulty; it may give little opportunity for attaining visible success; yet we know that constant fidelity in performing each daily duty, because it is God's will, draws down untold blessings ...'*

The dish of fried bread for Brother James's table was circulating slowly; James's heart sank — the slices seemed to be in shorter supply than usual. James could see that when Anselm had taken his slice there would be only one slice left on the dish, and how could Brother James take that while two confrères waited hungrily on his right flank? Oh the hewing and the hammering of the religious life! how narrow the cloisters and how thorny the gap that leads to eternal life! And yet there was the hundredfold promised, even in this life, to those who follow; a hundred slices of fried bread for every one offered up to the greater glory of the Lord!

Brother James sat back in surprise — Brother Anselm had taken both slices and had placed the empty plate in the centre of the long refectory table. Well! well! come follow me indeed! That would be several hundred slices knocked off his ration when — and if — he hit the plain deal tables of Heaven. The pig! struggling with the rest of them for the incorruptible crown — convinced that heaven will fill the cup of his happiness and spread before him the everlasting banquet of puddings, sausages and crisp, fried bread.

Anselm began to chew, tiny flakes of bread falling onto the table, the clacking harrow of teeth in the machine of Anselm's terrifying mouth beginning its work of destruction. Brother James wished to become the instrument of God's wisdom. A sudden jerk to the left struck the saintly elbow that was raising a mug of steaming tea towards the maw of Hell, and all the contents of the mug spilled out against Anselm's chest and down over his plate, drowning the evil lumps of bread, making its way through Anselm's soiled bib and darting its hot arrows into Anselm's shrivelled testicles. Anselm howled, and his chair skittered back across the wooden refectory floor.

After a stunned pause the novice took up the thread of his book:

' ... *It is not suggested that we will not feel the sting, that we will not smart under the humiliation, that we will find taking correction easy. See how we overcome our sensitive nature when we show ourselves to the surgeon and allow him to operate — we do likewise with the dentist. Let us also submit to the pain of correction. When we find nature boiling up, we should ask our Blessed Mother for help; when the tempest rages round thee, she will calm the troubled sea ...*'

'Amen!' thought Brother James, 'amen!'

* * *

Inevitably, ponderously, the terrible month of September had come round. Teachers and pupils, restored and shocked, went back underground. Three weeks into the term, Juniper, as usual, entered the staffroom and headed for his special corner. He flung his bag down under a chair and flopped into his usual place. 10.50 a.m., three classes over and he was already tired. Bored. Coffee break. After the break he had a free class. If Cleary were free, too, he might inveigle him into having a game of push-penny on the long table.

Other staff members came and went. There was a general huffing and blowing and sighing, bags and books being shifted and dropped, piles of copies — the corrected and the uncorrected — left in heaps here and there about the precious table or bundled without ceremony into lockers. Coffee break. One of the great institutions of teaching man. The great, aluminium boiler steaming away.

Juniper made his way over to the boiler. He dipped deep into the coffee tin, put a spoonful into the mug, a drop of milk, sugar; then, waiting his turn at the boiler he stirred it all into a creamy, light brown mess; this would help to give a sense of that Italian coffee that he loved — visions of Siena, Florence, San Gemigniano ... The dull matt walls of the staffroom. And there was Luke Flittermann talking to The Pants Moloney; two flat-arsed, flaky-skinned teachers of religion and economics; discussing the merits or demerits of some wholly indifferent pupil, or class; bless them!

Juniper took his coffee and went back to his chair; Cleary was there, flat out on his seat. Shluther O'Neill, Irish teacher, flopped down on Juniper's other side. Such glee! such unbounded glee! in life, and in one's avocation; such joy unbounded, such merriment unconfined!

'Ah Dukes,' Shluther sighed, 'hours to go yet, and those dumboes out there don't give a flute about a *síne fada* or a capital C. What's it all about, Dukes, answer me that?'

'Well, now, Shluther,' Cleary began, 'it's all about driving nails into your own head. If you spend your life doing that it's ten to one that you'll end up with a heavy head. The secret of life is to drive the nails into other peoples' heads.'

'Irony, irony,' Juniper punned.

'I'm going to chuck it all in,' Shluther went on, 'like Dukes here; take up law, have a soft life floating round the law library, getting other people to drive nails into each others' heads.'

This announcement again! never would, never could; and miles to go before I sleep, and miles to go ...

Juniper munched on his digestive, his thoughts on his boat. 'Sarah'. He would paint her white, and bring a fine blue strip all along the sides, looping it nicely at the bows and writing, in scarlet letters, SARAH, and then again across the stern, SARAH, Dublin.

'Ah, Dukes, to hell with you!' said Cleary, small and dapper, gentleman teacher, grinning and smirking like a wicked sinner. 'Only a few months for you, then you're off. Sometimes I think I even envy you.'

Vicarious pleasure they were taking from Juniper's scheme and yet he knew that deep down inside each one of them was the sheer gladness that they were not as crazy as he was, that they would never in their wildest moments make the first step to take themselves out of the rut they perpetually moaned about.

Juniper had spent the last class 'doing' Robert Burns. 'Oh my love is like a red, red rose ... ' It was on the Certificate course but he had spent the class reciting it for the boys, over and over, trying out a Scottish accent, trusting to his own relish for the poem to convey a love of it to the pupils before having to tear it to shreds before them. They had watched, and listened, open-eyed, open-eared, as Juniper recited the poem. They enjoyed the accent, they enjoyed the figure their teacher cut, but his hope was they would associate some enjoyment with a poem. For him, it was a more enjoyable way of spending fifty minutes. Later he would rip the poem open, apologising first to his pupils;

What is the theme of the poem?

Sum up the whole of life in one sentence.

Develop your detestation of poetry.

What is the poet *trying* to say?

Comment on the use of rhyme.

Put the roses down in mathematical terms, measure them, weigh them, judge the width of each petal, then say how much like the rose the poet's love really is.

Do you love the poem? If not, report to the headmaster after school.

Does the poem open your heart? give you goose-pimples? does it thrill your spine? do you have a spine?

If not, find out what's wrong at home, then read the poem again. If not yet, find out·what's wrong with your country, your school, yourself ...

After the class one of them, the slightly cross-eyed, gap-mouthed, curly-headed one they called 'Catgut' because he played the violin, sidled up to Juniper and handed him a sheet of paper, carefully folded.

'Please, sir, would you read that for me, sir?'

'What's this then? A ransom note?'

'No, sir, it's a poem, I wrote myself. I don't know if it's any good. I'd like for you to read it, please, sir.'

(Soon have all that nonsense creased out of you, Catgut. Won't get you that suburban semi with its two cars parked outside; not this way forward, Catgut, this way dreams, this way disappointment, this way gloom, this way freedom.)

'Of course I'll read it for you. I look forward to reading it.'

'But you won't let on, sir, please? I mean. Not in front of the class, like.'

'No, no, not at all; I'll keep it safe until after school.'

(Learning quickly enough, Catgut, learning; guard your dreams.)

Juniper finished his coffee. The door opened suddenly and Brother Canice came in, advanced a little into the staff-room, and stood, waiting. Bossman. Head-hunter. Portly. Certain. Bully. There was almost instant silence among the staff. For a moment, Juniper felt a pang of guilt, but he could not say why. To hell with him! there's the boat, Sarah, the sea ...

'May I have your attention a moment, please, gentlemen!'

A posture, this, his general aggression having already won him full attention. Revels in such moments.

'Just one or two small items, gentlemen ... '

The bad news first, announced with a definite leer ...

'I've noticed for some time that during the break the boys leave their books and copies and all their pencils and things higgledy-piggledy on their desks. Messy, gentlemen, messy. And things can, and things do, gentlemen, believe me, they do, get stolen. We haven't got a school full of saints here, you know, not all saints.'

Brother Canice chortled loudly, looking round at the poor, beleaguered staff. They say he has a glass eye. But which eye? One good eye, one glass eye, watching, watching ...

'So I wonder if the teacher who happens to be in a class when the bell goes for break wouldn't mind holding on a moment just to see that things are put away tidily. Shouldn't take more than a few seconds, I should think. Get the boys out first, shut the door, have everything all spickspan. Coffee will still be here for you, waiting. What do you say, gentlemen? shall we give it a try?'

How well he'd like to take them one by one and chew them up, spit them out onto the floor! The question remains, which eye? One eye brown, the other a sort of light brown with a hint of green to it. Hard to look into his eyes when you talk to him. One eye alive, one eye fixed. Dead. But which is which? No wonder he wins all arguments, has all his islanders cowed before the magic of his eye.

'Very good, gentlemen, very good. Now next Tuesday there is, as no doubt Brother Mark has told you, an important match against St Malachy's. This is the regional semi-final and we're hoping for a good deal of support at the game. I think we'll give a general half-day on Tuesday, allow every-one come along. Staff too. Of course.'

The bell rang.

'I won't hold you, gentlemen, from your classes ... '

But Juniper was able to sit on, restfully. The great joy of the teaching profession is the free class. There was a general scurrying among the staff, a gathering of instruments, maps, copies, rulers ... a mustering of energies and courage, perhaps, too, of aggression. Cleary sat on beside Juniper. A game of push-penny looked possible. Life was good. And there was, of course, Sarah, propped up at home, waiting ...

* * *

On Tuesday afternoon Juniper turned up at a great house on the south side of the city. A house of galleries and corridors, a house in which every room would have a musty smell; every room, that is, except those that admit the critical, finicky, but must-be-tolerated public. These rooms would be waxed, woeful and wondrous; the mahogany table, high-backed chairs designed to force the body into the most un-comfortable position possible; and against the heavily-ornate fireplace a fire-screen, with embroidered flowers, or a pranc-ing stallion, or a child's face with one large tear on the cheek signalling mourning over a broken doll. Juniper knew about such things, and he could imagine the black gondola-shoes of the priests, the layers of dust under each celibate bed, the drawers crammed with drawers, with notes for the definitive treatise on angels, mingling with a host of demure, thick socks. Oh no, none of your dinky-winky suburban houselets for these men, no clutter of yoghurt-smeared children to trip the feet and the mind, none of that here, here everything perfect and at peace. Where, oh where, have you been all your life?

Juniper shuddered himself out of that mood and rang the bell. Nothing happened. He pressed the button once more, and listened. Yes, a response in the remote distance, something like the awareness you have, in polite company, that your stomach has made an unwelcome sound and you wonder if everyone in the room has noticed. He shuffled a little on the gravel to overcome a surge of panic; what a ridiculous adventure this one was! dating agency, run from a seminary, what an absolute load of crushed cobblers that was and yet, perhaps that was the very reason he had chosen this particular route. Wholly impossible, implausible, laughable, crazy, preposterous. Worth a try.

He turned away from the huge white double-breasted door with its threatening fist of brass and its leering letterbox, and started back down the gravel driveway. Relief. Perhaps he should have gone to that match after all ... Then the door behind him opened and an old priest, bald, small, in floppy slippers, wearing an evilly green shirt under a grey-black pullover, called out after him.

'Did you want something?'

'I, aaammm,' — from twenty yards distant; 'it's OK Father, it's all right. Thanks all the same.'

'What did you say? Were you wanting something?'

'Well, yes, actually, I was going to meet Father Spaight at three o'clock. But it's OK, Father, don't worry about it.'

'Father Spaight, is it? Then it'll be the dating service you're about?'

This shout brought Juniper sharply back to the door; megaphone diplomacy, nerves overcome by more pressing dangers.

'That's is, Father, I was hoping, I, aaammm, yuh ... '

'Of course, of course, of course. A young man like yourself

should be married. Come on now, come in and I'll bring you down to Father Spaight's office. Yes, a good Catholic marriage is the best possible thing for a young man. Next, of course, to the blessed calling of the ministry.'

Juniper was led, by the elbow, and half-dragged, half-pushed inside; the door was closed behind him with a very definite sense of custodial authority. He was all knees and pockets and his nose began to water.

*   *   *

The 11.15 bus from Drogheda; Juniper met it at the bus station. He had been standing for some minutes before the bus drew in; he was brave, stolid, vehemently hating himself. Winnie. Winnie; a name somewhat staid and unexhilarating, and yet it could betoken someone round and jovial, with an inhibited raunchiness seeking self-expression. His belly tightened even more. Passengers began struggling down from the bus; the usual selection of human sufferers, the usual bags, the usual complaints. A very lovely girl with blonde and grey-streaked frizzed hair, wearing jeans and pink jumper insisting on a perfect body, descended, slowly, gazing round her; Juniper coughed and swallowed hard; Winnie? oh God has been known to be good beyond the craziest dreams of man! The girl moved away, into the bus station, Juniper gazing after her; she was greeted by an old man; passing in and out of Juniper's existence with so much potency and so little act.

'James Dukes?'

He turned back quickly. She was trim, wearing a grey suit, white blouse with suggestions of lace, a large grey handbag and yes, a scarf; plain-looking, definitely not young, definitely not designed with heart-stopping sex in mind. Juniper thought of denying the charge, of pretending to be waiting for someone else, of mistaking the bus. But he knew she must be in just as bad a shape as he was, to have gone through all the grids and gates and corrals he had gone through, and to get on a bus to meet the man the computer in a priest's office had decided would make the perfect partner for life. A sudden resentment, against the priest, against computers, and against himself if this is what he has been matched with, what does the computer say of him ... ?

'Aaaam, yes, Juniper, actually, I call myself. But yes, yes that's me, James Dukes. You must be Winnie?'

And of course if she was thirty-five wasn't Juniper thirty-five, too, and the sexy kittens weren't climbing the drainpipes to clamber into his bed. He took her arm, half overcome by the heavy talcum scent from her clothes or body, and steered her through the station and out into the battle-ground of Saturday morning Dublin.

They had a drink in the Abbey Mooney's, to loosen things a bit. In there it was cool and dim and empty.

'What'll it be, Winnie? How about a brandy to start us off?'

'Not for me, thanks, James, I don't touch alcohol. But you must feel free to go ahead, if you like.'

'Oh, I see, aaammm, yes, OK, coffee then? How about a cup of coffee?'

'Yes, please, James, that'll be grand.'

'Yes, and aaammm, I'll just have a little Irish, then, and please do call me Juniper, I prefer that.'

Then the DART to Bray, the lovely Dublin coastline on the left, the strand at Merrion, the sparkle of sunlight on platform tiles, the wading birds indifferent to the passing train, and figures far out on the strand digging for lug-worm. The bay at Killiney, the long descent into Bray station, the sea, the sky, the golf-course, people moving about in their colours and their certainties, and Juniper sliding through the world on a lake of ice. Having to make conversation changed the pain; the knot in his stomach did not ease, even after a second whiskey. Initial conversation was simple enough, factual, hardly probing; she was a primary school teacher (bloody computer again!) first class this year, second class next; had her own wee flat in Fair Street, often cycled out to the sea at Mornington, or over to Newgrange, or even out to the old ruins of Monasterboice. She spoke quietly, but he knew that she, too, was strained.

After Dalkey the carriage was almost empty; she shifted once on the seat opposite him and crossed her legs; for the first time he was stirred, she had good legs indeed, and the amount of thigh revealed was distinctly shapely. Juniper shifted, too, self-consciously, but she didn't reach for the hem of her skirt to pull it tighter. He wished they could just stop talking, let the rhythm of the train soothe them, watch together the changing aspect of the sea; he wished he could stare with full freedom at her legs and thighs, imagining all that there was further inside that dark tunnel, or even kneel before her at once and let his words flood all over her, opening his life at once, telling her; if only they could get rid, at once, of that awful sexual urge, that curiosity, if he could just shuck from him the years' accretions of diffidence and self-awareness, then there would be a chance of getting to know her without that perpetual strain between them ...

She talked quickly, staccato, emphatic sentences; about the children, the syllabus, pollution, video nasties ... They ate at a simple café on the seafront, the sun forcing Juniper towards two pints of cider. Where she put all those cups of coffee he could only wonder. They sat on the stones along the beach, she settling her skirt stiffly before she sat down; it was not comfortable, but it was warm. There were long periods of silence between them which Juniper tried to hide by throwing stones into the sea, by naming any of the seabirds that came close to shore, by avoiding any of the questions she asked him about himself.

He wondered if he should mention the boat? he felt she would not be able for that. Yet there was the merest sense of some remote possibility between them that kept him cautious still, even hopeful. Yet there had been no real contact yet between them, he knew he was not allowing any real contact, and that all he was able to do was think of her as a sexual being, desirable, but obviously unattainable, at least he felt she was living sexually very far away, behind the hope of marriage and 'settling down'.

He lay back down into his old, medieval darkness, down on the stones, shuffling his body to try and ease his shape among them; he put his hands behind his head and looked up at the blue, chilling sky. She was gifted with a fine back, too, her dark hair could almost be beautiful over the nape of her neck. She had fallen silent; now she lay back, too, close to him, her head almost against his shoulder, nestling into the stones, nudging her body closer to his. He felt now that if he put his right arm under her head she would snuggle in against him, out of her need, into his: that then something would be allowed to germinate, quickly, between them, something true and real and believable. He hesitated; and quickly the moment passed, making it impossible for him now to reach her. They lay awhile, the silence different between them, sadder, and conclusive.

She wanted to go home by the 6.15 bus; they both knew there was another bus at 11.00. At the station he felt a sudden rush of affection for her, or was it pity? or even pity for himself? Where has she been all her adult life? She had been gentle, thoughtful, and open with him; he had kept her at a distance. At the bus door she turned back towards him and he put his arms about her and kissed her on the lips with quiet gentleness. It was their first contact. She was not surprised; she looked into his eyes for a moment; her arms clung compulsively to him and she tightened them about his waist; there was a momentary fire in her eyes, some impulse of anger, pain, resentment, and he knew the fire was not aimed at him; she kissed him, too, and her hand moved down and gripped his buttocks as she pulled him towards her, tightly. Then she was on the steps of the bus, waiting to show her ticket to the driver.

'Bye, Juniper, and thanks for a lovely day.'

† † †

Brother Theo Higgins was so tall and skinny he could barely hold himself erect. His red hair, though he was barely twenty years of age, was already thin and his unhandsome face was pocked and acneyed. He wore rimless glasses which kept slipping down to the tip of his nose. When he togged out for games he was a strange sight indeed; he stayed enthusiastically clear of the ball and would willingly stop his roving about the field to discuss the psalms or some of the less harmful figures of the Old Testament. Brother Ostrich, the Brothers named him as they watched him make an ungainly lunge for the ball long after it had safely passed him by. In all things else Brother Theo was a model, devout, serious, a stickler for every detail of the rule. He seemed, indeed, to embody that invisible goal of novitiate perfection to which all were supposed to run.

It came as a shock to Brothers Andrew, Luke and James when, late one evening, the Novice Master beckoned to them, one by one, as they filed out of the Chapel after Vespers. When they had divested they followed the Master down a corridor, through the heavy door that led from the postulants' quarters to the priests' residence. A small thrill of fear and astonishment, of apprehension, ran through Brother James to find himself in an area strictly out of bounds to the young and unprofessed. Everything seemed brighter here, the walls with lighter tones of paint than the excremental brown and dark cabbage green of the postulants' rooms. Each door sported a traffic-light signal outside; knock or ring and the saint within pressed his button — green light, enter;

orange light, wait a moment; red light, piss off!

Astonishment grew as the Master, tall as a reed and as thin, with high owl-like face and branch-sharp features, paused before one such door, gathered his three lambs about him and spoke gravely and quietly;

'Now Brothers, Brother Theo has become somewhat unwell; we have had to have the doctor look at him. He is perfectly all right, physically, but has become a little disturbed and the doctor has had to give him something to calm him down. Tomorrow he will go to the hospital but tonight he will rest in this room; I want you three to stay and watch with him.'

'Watch what?' James blurted out.

'Watch over him, Brother James, watch over him. He is asleep and will probably sleep all night, but he may try to move, or he may come slightly awake and talk a little, foolish things, disturbed things. So you will please watch over him, soothe him if he speaks, though doctor assures me he will sleep deeply. Please stay until I come back to you, which I will do before Matins. Three of you will ensure that, even if one sleeps for a while, the others shall watch; turn and turn about, you may, of course, sleep.'

The Brothers had become even more terrified; the Master opened the door and they went in. Theo was in bed, there was a pale, amber night-light in a corner of the room; it amplified and magnified the presence that was hovering. James began to remember some of the horror movies he had seen, the play of the imagination on all the possible and impossible aberrations that humanity may be prey to, the palms of his hands grew damp, the rest of his body chilled, a throbbing pain began somewhere in the well of his stomach. An older Brother had been sitting near the head of the bed and he now left, at a nod from the Master. The Master then beckoned the three novices to sit down and he left, quietly, without another word.

The Brothers looked at each other, each ashen-faced and stiff. At first James imagined that Theo was dead, that this was in fact a wake, that some dreadful manifestation of the presence of Satan would take place in the unholy hours of the morning, the soul of Theo being a special one, Satan would clearly make a bid for that soul. But Theo, from the bed, snorted, his whole body jerked as if smitten by a sudden shock; the three postulants sat up straight, terrified; Theo's breathing settled down again; he slept on. It had just gone nine o'clock, it was dark outside, dawn was a very, very long way away.

After Theo had lain wholly still for some minutes, James, Andrew and Luke relaxed a little. Luke took out his rosary beads and began to pass them slowly between his fingers. The amber light seemed to have strengthened in the room as the darkness deepened outside. James began to feel some pride in the thought that the Master had chosen him for a responsible job like this. But that way lay the awful sin, and Satan was hovering in the room; he remembered Peter, James and John, (James!), another trio asked to stay and watch, in a special garden, and how they had failed ... He felt for the beads in his own pocket, but he left them there. Instead he whispered to Andrew:

'Do you think the rule of Great Silence applies to us here, too, I mean while we're on this job?'

Andrew replied quickly; 'I wouldn't think so. We'll have to be able to talk if Theo gets stroppy. Anyway, we can't read in this light so we'll have to talk or we'll all go as nutty as poor old Theo.'

'Do you think he's really barmy? Nuts? Mad, like?'

'Poor worm, thou art infected,' quoted Andrew; then he added, 'Of course he's nuts; he's had a nervous breakdown. Too much praying, no relaxation. He's just burst. Gone fffwhoooosh! just like that! Topped. Cracked. Holed.'

James fell silent under the weight of this thought. He had

never seen anyone collapse before. It didn't look too good. Theo was twitching slightly, his forehead puckering, his fingers jerking, as if some living thing, independent of the man himself, were leaping about inside his skin.

'Possessed,' James said in awe, 'that must be what it is. He's possessed by some evil spirit. There'll be an exorcism.'

'Possessed my arse!' retorted Luke. 'The poor eejit's lost his marbles. Too much tension in him. Like a fiddle that's been tuned too tightly. No give. Following the Rules without any imagination. No leeway. Bound to snap. Anyway, spirits and possession and all that, that's all rubbish.'

'The isle is full of noises!' muttered Andrew.

Outside in the corridor a grandfather clock chimed the quarter hour. There was a real world beyond that door. In the room the postulants shifted to make themselves more comfortable on their hard chairs. Theo slept and twitched, inhabiting his own world. All the others would be in bed by now, most of them already asleep. God would be watching from his own place, watching over the world, testing souls, gathering up the fallen, turning his back on his chosen ones to get them to love him even more. Maybe that's what was happening to poor Theo. Maybe he was a special saint, like John of the Cross, or Teresa of Avila — Theo of Mullingar!

After each postulant had travelled the byways of the rosary at least twice, the grandfather clock had chimed the half-hour. There was a long way to go yet. Luke began to tell a ghost story. James listened for a while, but when he began to feel a chill about his back and had looked askance over his shoulder a few times, he told Luke to cut it out. They had enough to cope with without ghost stories. At last the deep, resonant 'drronnnnnnngs' of the clock marked the hour. In the amber cavern where the sick postulant lay, the clock sounded loud and threatening. Each quarter seemed as long as an hour to the young watchers. Theo remained calm, turning occasionally, a complex manoeuvre from right side to left side, back from left side to right; he did not waken, he appeared, as the night advanced, less disturbed. There was a long, long period of silence.

James was in a lovely state of half-sleep, his head drooping forward and then jerking to bring consciousness hovering at a polite distance, while he allowed the half-dreams to take him over. Then he became aware that Luke was chuckling to himself.

'Hey, Brother James,' Luke whispered, 'a thought has just struck me. You know, you and I, and no doubt Brother Andrew here, and without a shadow of a doubt poor blessed Theo on his bed of pain, we're all virgins! Virgins! Can you beat that? Virgins, isn't that a thought for you? Look at us, for Christ's sake, three virgins watching a fourth virgin pirouetting into cuckoo land! I ask you!'

'For Christ's sake indeed!' thought James, 'that sums it up.' He grinned a little sheepishly at Luke, not being terribly certain what exactly was meant by being a virgin. He thought he was a virgin, indeed, if masturbation didn't count, but it was not a virginity acquired by a great deal of suffering and struggle, but rather virginity by default. Yet James was well aware of the attraction of a woman's body, how being separated for life from the possibility of enjoying a woman's body can bring a catch of despair to the heart. Why, he wondered, had God created something so abjectly longed for and then made its possession so difficult, made the possessor of the longed-for object so intent on both displaying and withholding the treasure that it becomes one more proof of the cruelty, ingenious and malicious, of a leering God? 'For Christ's sake' — truly!

James shifted uneasily. Dangerous thoughts. Fens. Marshes. Avoid them. Underneath the heavy brown fabric of the habit he could feel already the stirrings of an erection. That was sin, that was torture to the poor virgin, merit, if it can be resisted, that hundredfold promised to those who ...

And again James was thinking of the hundredfold, imagining a hundred women offering themselves to his pleasure for every woman he had avoided in this life, rejecting them for the sake of Heaven. But no, no, no, because in Heaven there would be no bodies, there would be no sex, no difference between male and female, so he would never know, down the endless, bright corridors of eternity, never taste a woman's body, never even have the ...

Brother Theo was getting out of bed. In silence, with slow and deliberate movements he reached one long leg onto the floor and was heaving the other out after it. James was the first to become aware of the movement; he froze in terror. Theo was sitting on the edge of the bed, watching, not seeing the postulants. He began to take off the top of his pyjamas. The three virgins moved together. Andrew was the first to reach the bed.

'Now, Brother Theo, we must not get up just yet. We must try and get some sleep, until morning. There's a good man now. Back into bed, there's a good man.'

Theo did not appear to notice. He had the top of the pyjamas off and was gazing about him for his clothes. His eyes, wide open, were unlike any eyes James had ever seen. They were frightening in their slow, mechanical shifting about, glazed, like glass balls, unblinking, servants to some unreal and distant world. Theo stood up, groped about at the foot of the bed, then began to head towards the door.

Quickly Brother Luke was at his elbow, holding him; 'It's all right, Brother Theo, it's all right now. Not time to get up yet. It's just after Compline, we've all got to go to bed now, we'll just say night prayers with you, then we'll all go to bed.'

Theo looked at him, did not recognise him, ignored his very existence. Then he began to take off his pyjama bottoms. The three Brothers stood at a loss. Theo was naked, his gangling, stooping body hairless and white, apart from a tiny tuft of red pubic hair, his body more skin and knuckle than was possible to believe, vulnerable as a dried-out twig and governed now by something far beyond the scope of the young virgins to name. He began to make for the door.

'Oh no!' James shouted, and he rushed to the door and put his back to it, spreading out his arms like crucified Jesus.

'Excuse me, please,' the words came slowly from Theo's chest. 'I must go now.'

'Where?' James asked desperately. 'Where do you have to go?'

'Murtagh's. Kerosene. Mother wants some. I must go.'

He reached past James for the handle of the door. James gripped it first.

'You have no clothes on, Theo, you can't go out naked, you must go back to bed till morning. Anyway, Murtagh's is closed.'

Theo gripped James's hand, and James was astonished at the coldness and power of the hand.

'Kerosene. I must get some. Now.'

His voice was beginning to rise; he went on mumbling the word, kerosene, over and over, the voice becoming shrill. His hand began to force James to turn the handle of the door and he was stronger by far than James. By now Luke and Andrew were at the door too and it took all their strength to keep it closed. Then Theo simply stopped, looked at them as if about to strike out at them. There was anguish written on his face but his eyes were still as dead as glass beads. He sank to the floor, squatted on his knees and began rocking himself backwards and forwards. Without words. Without sobs. A slow rocking in the sickly light of the cave.

He looked up towards the curtains, got up and headed slowly towards the window. They were three floors up.

'Fuck!' said Brother Luke and he and Theo got to the window together.

'James,' Andrew hissed, 'go and get Brother Moloney, quickly, we'll never manage this.'

James opened the door and at once Theo was rushing

towards it, away from the window. Luke leaped on his back and held him round the shoulders, Andrew dived like a rugby player and took him about the knees. All four fell to the floor and James kicked the door shut. The three postulants gathered themselves up carefully, Theo stayed on the floor, on his side, rolled himself up foetally, and grew still.

'Jesus we've killed him, or knocked him out maybe.'

'No, he's OK, a bit stunned maybe, see, he's shivering.'

'He'll get his death of cold like that.'

Theo was shivering, his eyes still open, hands joined over his genitals, knees drawn up against his chest.

'She'll kill me, she'll kill me. It's not my fault. I was asleep, I swear. I won't do it again. I didn't know. It's not my fault. Look, my pyjamas, they're dry, look ... ' and he began to feel over his naked body for his pyjamas.

'Here,' said Luke, 'here they are Brother Theo,' and he held out the pyjamas towards him. Theo did not seem to notice, he did not seem to hear.

'My hands are dry, look, dry. Everything is dry. I couldn't have, don't you see? Don't you believe me? Please, please ... '

Andrew muttered from behind the other two;

'This is a strange repose, to be asleep, with eyes wide open; standing, speaking, moving, and yet so fast asleep.'

'Oh shut up with your Shakespeare, Andrew,' Luke hissed.

'Quick, Luke,' whispered James, 'what's his name? What's Theo's real name, before he came in here, I mean?'

'I think it was Peter,' Luke said. 'Peter Higgins.'

'Here, Peter,' James said, taking the pyjamas and holding them out to him. 'Here's your pyjamas, Peter, and they're perfect, dry as bone. See? Here, put them on before you die of the cold.'

Theo took the pyjamas from him and the three Brothers helped him get them on and got him back into bed. He went easily, quietly, and was asleep at once. They waited some

time before they sat down again, drawing their chairs closer
to the bed, closer to each other, smiling with relief, straight-
ening their habits, finding themselves back in a world that
was almost real once more. The night moved on. Outside, in
the corridor, the clock told them midnight. Gradually they
drew back into the shell of silence that was growing about
them through the corridors and cells of the novitiate, a safety
for each of them, setting each apart from the others, creating
individual souls incapable of knowing each other and incapable of knowing himself. But Theo's shell had cracked and
the snail-soft flesh was exposed; the way a thrush smashes
and cracks the shell against its special stone until the raw,
vulnerable goodness appears on the hard surface of the
world.

* * *

Juniper began to spend time on his boat. He had propped her
up on wooden supports in the garage; he had light and
warmth and could work into the night, oiling and cleaning
the motor, painting within and without, outfitting the cabin
with comfortable furnishings, gas stove, bunk beds. He had
one of the beds fastened and mattress, blankets, pillow in
position.

One evening in late October he tried the motor; he had put
in just one gallon of fuel, allowed it to percolate through the
engine, then, his heart fluttering, he tried the switch. At first
— nothing; a click, not even a cough. Then he remembered
the battery — he wired that up, and tried again. The engine
purred into life at once, a soft, powerful sound. His sense of
elation was enormous. He could hear the cocks crowing from
the summits of old Italian towns. He could hear staff and
pupils cheering him on his way. He ran next door, to tell
Marie-Claire, and Brendan.

Marie-Claire brought him into her kitchen. Brendan was

away for the week, she told him, some specialist tour of archaeological sites.

'Do stay a while, Cheemy, and tell me your plans.'

Juniper told her, outlining his hopes for escape from his dead-end life.

'But we will all miss you, Cheemy. What will we do without you in the house next door?' She began to make him a cup of coffee.

Juniper would be glad to escape from the sounds that came through the wall but he did not tell her that. The occasional view he had of her in her back garden on warm summer days when she'd lie out in her bikini to take the sun — that wasn't too easy on him, either. Juniper had often imagined himself as Jupiter, god of the sun, reaching a hot tongue down and moving it slowly all over that luscious, warming body. He didn't tell her that either.

'And Italy, Cheemy, how do you know you will like Italy? Have you ever been there? do you know anybody there?'

'Well no, I don't know anyone but I have been in Italy before, went on a tour to Rome, then out to places like Naples and Sorrento, up as far as Venice. I want to spend a few days in Assisi over the Hallowe'en break.'

If someone were to ring her up now and tell her that her Brendan had had an accident, that she was a widow ... she would need consoling, he would have a duty to ... How could one leave such a young, full body unattended, such an open, generous spirit without comfort? The widow Dido. But the phone did not ring. Juniper knew the phone would never ring.

She brought him over a cup of coffee and asked him if he might not like to have something with it?

'No, thank you, no, this is lovely, and I'll have to get back to *Sarah*.'

She giggled.

'You have a girlfriend waiting for you in your little house?'

'Oh no, no such luck, I'm afraid. Sarah is the name of the boat.'

'Sarah is such a lovely name, Cheeemy, but of course you would have all of us jealous, if you had a little girl in there with you.'

She was smiling down at him; he sat at the end of the table, sipping a very hot cup of coffee. She was lovely in jeans and blouse, frighteningly lovely, disturbing.

'And the engine does seem to be working, so now I must try her out in the sea one day soon.'

'Oh Cheeeeemy, that sounds very, very dangerous. Is there not a lake or a river you could start in, to be safe?'

'Well, there is actually, a friend of mine has a boat on the river Boyne, and he asked me to bring Sarah up there some day. I might just do that.'

A great wail came from upstairs.

'Oh, Cheemy, please excuse me, that's Nicole. I'll just settle her down and come back. Do not stir now, please. OK?'

Juniper sat drinking his coffee, a great swell of happiness passing over him; the comfort of his present situation, the knowledge of the boat waiting, the prospects ... all was well, all manner of things would be well. Then she was back, just she and he, alone together, a lovely woman, with him, in her house, late evening ...

She came round his chair and as she did so her hand brushed his hair lightly, as a mother might do to her child, affectionately, proudly.

'She's OK, Nicole, just a little wakeful. So now, Cheemy, you will be leaving Seawood Court. And who will I have to be thinking about during the long empty days?'

Oh my God, oh my holy God!

'Oh I'm sure I won't be missed from the Court, nor from the school, nor from the whole blessed island!'

'Oh yes, Cheeeemy, I will miss you, I will, I will.'

She came towards him, put her hand on his shoulder and

stood looking down into his face. He was aware of her breasts just a few inches from his eyes, her thigh was pressing against his elbow. Then she bent and kissed him lightly on the forehead. Oh Lord. She took his head between her hands and gazed down into his eyes. Those soft, green eyes, deep and lovely and challenging. Juniper didn't know where to look.

'There is no need to be lonely, Cheemy, you know? No-one must be lonely in this world. Do you understand, Cheeeemy?'

She kissed him again, a lingering kiss, full on the lips. Juniper was not able to respond. He was frozen. He did not know how to respond. His glasses slipped down onto the tip of his nose. She kept kissing him. Then she turned and was on his lap, her firm flesh heavy and heavenly on his knees, she was sitting on his knees, and she was kissing him. Him! Juniper!

He was terrified. And excited. She stood then, holding his hand and gently drawing him up from the chair.

'Come, Cheemy, come, let's go upstairs, just for once, just this evening. Let's make love together, now, before you go and leave us. There is no need for us ever to be alone and lonely, Cheemy, there is no need ... '

Juniper stood and looked at her as if she were a ghost; he was unable to move. He thought of his feet, of his socks, were they clean ... ? what would he do? how do you ... ?

'But perhaps you do not like me, Cheemy, is that it?'

'Oh no, no, not at all. I mean, of course I like you. Maybe even I love you. I don't know.'

'Eh bien, that is all right so?'

And she was drawing him towards the kitchen door. Then upstairs? and then ... ?

'But your husband ... ? Brendan. I mean, you're married ... and I, I mean ... '

'I know that, Cheeemy. I am sure Brendan is not always faithful to me when he is away for long weeks. I get lonely, too, Cheemy, and I am sure you are lonely sometimes?'

'Yes, indeed, oh yes. Often. But, I, ... '

'Oh Cheemy you are afraid of me? have you not ever made love with a married woman before?'

'Of course I have. It's not that. It's just, I mean, if it was ... '

She was pulling him towards the door, tugging at him as you would tug at a mule in the middle of the road. Then there was silence. She grew tired of it.

'Oh well, then, Cheemy, that's all right. Maybe you should go back to your lovely Sarah, eh? Go back now to your Sarah, and good night, Cheemy.'

Juniper rushed out the back door and round the side of the house, into the garage where he banged shut the heavy door, climbed into the boat, and stretched out on the bunk, shuddering and trembling. He cursed himself, he despised and loathed himself. What a fool! How hopeless, how absolutely hopeless! And yet somewhere he knew that he was right; but why? where could the harm be? How wonderful it would have been. How incredibly beautiful and revealing and breathtaking it could have been. That lovely body, on the rubber ocean, naked, his. But Brendan! he didn't give a damn about Brendan. He lay on the bunk and cursed himself into tears.

As he lay, quieting his poor body and his red-sore brain, trying to ease the hurt, he called up to himself a plethora of lovely women. He was Prospero, and all the spirits came at his behest, building out of the air a mansion draped in scarlet hangings, an enormous waterbed in the centre and there he was, Juniper-Prospero, afloat. The women came in all their lovely nakedness, blonde, brunette, from Africa and Brazil and Bangkok, shifting round him, ministering to him. Some of them poured wine all over him and he took great draughts of it as it washed over his face; some of them pressed fruits on him, melons and bananas and peaches; some scattered flower petals over his warm, wine-moistened body, while they caressed and fondled him, climbing over him where he lay in total passivity, accepting their offerings, breathing in the fragrances of their bodies. He was unable to prolong the vision. He was too excited, he was overwrought, and as he brought himself that poor, momentary relief, the visions fled; he was enclosed again in the small, dim cabin of his boat, afloat only on the garage floor, the lovely Marie-Claire in the house next door thinking ill of him. Oh this island, this Ireland, this mind, this island!

'Our revels now are ended,' he said to himself, climbing wearily down from the boat, vowing to speed up the whole business and escape from the estate where he could find no peace.

* * *

It was evening. Juniper was full of words about his hopes, his boat. He was in 'The Bull's Mouth' with Richard Hartwood, an English teacher from another school. Richard was one of those rare souls whose view of life was uncankered in spite of all that the greed and selfishness of the twentieth century could do to him. He, too, had ambitions to produce a volume of poetry that would be read; he, too, taught English literature as if it were not the insides of a computer; he was the only one who had encouraged Juniper in his plan of escape. They had been chatting for over an hour; the pub was full and both of them were feeling airy. Two women came into the pub; they were at a loss as to where to find space; Juniper pushed Richard over and beckoned them to their table. They sat down, smiling, but immediately made moves to consolidate their position as a remote, uninterested, separate party.

The conversation between Richard and Juniper grew more animated. One of the women went to the bar to get drinks; the two men talked of the possibilities of earning money teaching English in towns like Bari, Naples, even on Capri;

Juniper's eye was on the young woman who had gone to buy the drinks; she was beautiful, raven-haired, sexy, disturbing. Juniper chided himself for noticing; his guilt over Marie-Claire had left him even more wary, yet his wariness also seemed to confer an indifference, a submission to the belief that he would never find a woman or sexual fulfillment.

The evening wore on; the pub was hot and noisy; Richard got up to go to the toilet; almost at the same time the other woman got up to go to the bar for drinks; Juniper was left alone with the raven. Almost at once she called across to him: 'It's very hot in here, isn't it?'

Juniper plunged;

'Yes, it's like a furnace. No wonder they call it the Bull's Mouth!'

Her eyes were a dark brown, suggesting to Juniper a wooded glade where rabbits frisked freely among ferns and berries and where sunlight slanted onto the boles of trees. She smiled, her teeth were wonderfully white, her raven hair framed her face to perfection. He swallowed hard.

'Can I get you a drink?'

'No thanks. Sue has gone to the bar. The service here isn't too great.'

'No, it's not.'

They were shouting to each other across the table. There was a pause. Was that it?

'Any interest in the match today?' Juniper hazarded.

She shook her head.

'No thank you,' she shouted, 'I don't smoke.'

Juniper laughed. And to explain himself he pulled his chair round to be closer to hers. And she laughed, too. Oh that blue sheen that lived and danced in her black hair. Then Sue came back. There was such a sudden show of disappointment on Juniper's face that the raven laughed again.

'Why don't you both come closer, round beside us?' she suggested, 'then we can all chat.'

Richard came back to an altered situation; Juniper was deep in conversation with one woman, and her young, fair-haired companion was clearly expecting Richard to engage her in chat. Oh Juniper, Juniper, what a wonder, Juniper!

After so many years, then, it came as easy as that! and Sarah was her name, Sarah McNulty, from Dublin, a teacher. Conversation was easy; Juniper and Sarah spoke animatedly of trivial things. Of course he told her about the boat; she laughed at the name and marvelled that someone could give up teaching for a mad caper on the oceans of the world. She probed so much she invited her to Seawood Court to have a look at the boat for herself. Would she? She'd be delighted. So there he was writing out his address in her small, scented notebook.

* * *

It was Saturday afternoon, one of those early winter days with the city enveloped in smog, the air still. Where Juniper lived, close to the sea, there was a slight breeze, the holy spirit working its way along the coastline. Boats were visible out on the estuary, moored, perfectly poised on their own reflections, the tiny stirring of the water caused by the breeze and the scarcely perceptible movement of the tide. He was in the garage, doors closed against the world, against Marie-Claire. He was varnishing the interior wood of the cabin and there was a strong, almost overwhelming smell from the paint.

He was lucky to hear the doorbell late in the afternoon. He scrambled out of the boat and opened the garage door; Sarah stood, with her back to him, at the hall door! He was able to compose himself, astonished and delighted at her presence. He gazed at her, stunned once again by her sensuous body, her full figure, her elegant height. He called out to her. Now it was she who was startled but her laughter rang out clear and bubbly and she smiled a smile that made a Provençal noon out of the suburban gloom.

They sat over a glass of wine in the kitchen, Juniper somewhat abashed by the state of his painting clothes and the general, customary untidiness of his batchelor home. Sarah explained she had been at the airport to leave her parents off. They were catching a flight to Marbella; would spend a three week holiday. She thought she might come home via Malahide, on the odd chance of seeing Juniper's boat.

He brought her out to the garage; they brought the wine. She laughed a good deal over the boat. He showed her charts and pictures he had gathered for his trip to the promised land. She sat on the bunk and Juniper sat on a stool at the other side of the cabin. They chatted easily and he was pleased to find himself relaxed in her company. Then suddenly she got up to go, banging her head against the low shelf above her. Juniper leaped to the rescue and held her about the shoulders, cautiously but firmly. She was still laughing and said she would love to be able to throw away the teaching life if she had the courage. Another dream began to take shape in Juniper's brain. Soon, perhaps, some day soon, please God, please God, he might broach it. She invited him to come to her house the following day, Sunday, for lunch. Would he come? It would give her the impetus to cook a proper meal now that her parents were away. And she'd be happy to see him again. She wasn't a great cook. But would he come? Please? *Would he come!*

She climbed down the ladder to the garage floor, then she was gone. Juniper remained in a stupor of happiness. He climbed back into the dimly lit cabin where she had been, where she had spent perhaps a half hour with him. Her scent was there, delicate, definite. He touched the bunk where she had been sitting, then buried his face in the memory of her presence. Now, he thought, I must not, I must not muck this one up.

† † †

The study-cum-library was shared by postulants, novices and Brothers alike. It was the hold of a great steamer, laden with desks in ordered rows, shelves of books along the side walls and around the back, cases reaching from floor to ceiling, an overwhelming cargo of knowledge to be crammed into one tiny, monastic head. Brother Boniface was librarian.

Brother James sat in the library, reading the Rules and Constitution of the order, and he gazed upon these rows and rows of books, those accessible to all, those high above, those locked away out of reach. There, he thought, must be contained all the knowledge in the world, all the knowledge of the flesh and of the devil. Rumours were always going about that some of these books outlined the great and soul-destroying secrets revealed only to the sinful Popes of History, the detailed words and phrases that would consti-tute the unforgivable sin, the texts revealed to the plump Doctor of the Church, which he could and would only write down in a code known to himself alone, and to God, because their revelation must impel all men to suicide.

It was said, too, that the terrible books of necromancy were here, books revealed by Satan himself when he used the heretics as his instruments; books, too, on the human body, on female anatomy, illustrated manuals on sex — for the instruction of those very special confessors and spiritual directors dealing directly with sinful humankind — that *Lady Chatterly's Lover* was chuckling away to itself somewhere up there and — for those most mature of students who were called upon, under obedience, to be able to counter the criminal elements of the literary world, *Ulysses* by the terrible James Joyce.

Brother James was scared of these subjects, but he would work to become an expert, too, in a special area, he would take notes, develop his understanding, his exegesis, and perhaps succeed in adding another volume to the shelves; *Reflections on Mariology in the Light of Contemporary Eschatology*, by the Reverend James A. Dukes, DD, MA, PhD. He would dedicate himself and all his honours and successes to Mary, selflessly give all he was to her, body, soul, torments, joys, to be her special lover for ever and she would be his Muse, his deity, his star. He would pray, head down between his hands lest his fellow postulants should see his fervour and force him to commit even the most venial sin of spiritual pride:

'I, James A. Dukes, a faithless sinner, renew and ratify today in thy hands, O Immaculate Mother, the vows of my baptism. I renounce for ever Satan, his works and pomps, and I give myself entirely to Jesus Christ, thy Son, to carry my cross after him all the days of my life and to be more faithful to him than I have ever been before ... '

Outside the library windows sparrows were chattering and arguing in the dust. Brother James breathed in deeply, marvelling at the special privilege he had been accorded of being a chosen servant, a holy monk, a sanctified soul, a devotee of the Holy, Immaculate Muse.

Later that night, on the hard bed in his cell, Brother James found it difficult to sleep. It was shortly after ten o'clock, there was still brightness in the sky. There was a thrush singing somewhere, shattering the silence of the monastery as you would shatter a glass. Brother James could feel the light of evening reach through the frayed curtain towards him, wishing to draw back his blanket, draw off the nightshirt, lead him out into the coolness of the night, carry him into its demanding embrace.

James switched himself over on the bed and began to say the rosary, running the words together in a rhythm to lull him into sleep. But from somewhere, perhaps from the very spines of those books on the high shelves, floated in a thought, bursting the images he tried to raise of Jesus in the

Holy Land, breaking through all the birdsong and the light; the thought: I wonder what it would be like if I were a sex symbol for my time?

He saw himself, brown habit gone, he stood in expensive, designer casuals, hip-huggers, testicle-emphasisers; no button on the shirt, just leather thongs loosely criss-crossing a chest of fine, dark hair; slung down over that chest a delicate golden cross on a delicate golden chain. Now he was leaning languidly against a bar in the foyer of a Dublin hotel, or perhaps it was New York, or Paris, or Amsterdam, while the women gathered around him, hoping for his favours, a glance, an autograph, a hair from his wicked chest, a hair from his classic head, a hair...

James switched himself back in the bed and began the third mystery of the joyful, all over again. His nightshirt was coarse, it itched and irritated the flesh whenever he stirred, for the glory of God and for the taming of Brother Ass, Amen! He was hot, he twisted the beads tightly between his fingers and whispered his prayers into the thickening air of his room.

To have a special car, a Mercedes sport for example, three short-skirted women on the front seat beside him, their heads thrown back in the pride and pleasure of his company, their breasts generous, half-exposed, their thighs bare just below the level of the steering-wheel, and he drives through the trendy streets of Mayfair to a party in someone's penthouse flat, wine and champagne, music and conversation. There is a lull followed by a burst of applause as James appears at the appartment door, one of the women holding it open for him, another taking his leather jacket, the third already gone in search of the choicest cocktail sausages for him, a glass of champagne to wash them down. They will clear a bed for him down a dark-blue corridor, a large round bed, lewd paintings on the walls, the ceiling one vast mirror, and he will fling himself down on the bed with a sigh, patiently allowing his three attendants to undress him and ... Glory be to the Father and to the Son and to the Holy Ghost ...

Brother James got out of bed and washed his face in cold water in the basin. He held his face under for as long as he could, then let the water drop back into the basin. He drew the curtain and peered down into the yard; it was darker now, the stable doors shut, not a sound to be heard. The cobbles shone with a glow from the rising moon and he could see tufts of grass growing among the cobblestones. No-one about, nobody but himself to cope with, his own weight and presence, his mind, his body.

He moved about the tiny room for a while, trying to pace himself into some form of sleepiness, then he got back into bed. He settled himself as comfortably as he could, assuming confidence, hoping to fool himself into sleep. Start the routine of night prayers all over again, concentrate on the words ... I lay my body down to sleep, and pray to God my soul to keep, and there was a wrestling ring, somewhere out under the sun, on a deserted beach, James in the red corner, naked; in the blue corner, also naked, a big, beautiful woman, heavy-weight, and the bell was ringing and she had him in a bear-hug, his head crushed hard into her breasts and then she had flung him onto the canvas and had thrown herself on top of him, the full weight of her body on him as she heaved his shoulders back, and he was panting and heaving and she was up again and had lifted him and thrown him against the ropes and he had fallen again, and she was on top of him once more, leaping onto his stomach, pinning him down with her weight, and then she was crawling all over him, rising to sit astride his chest, pressing him to the canvas with her whole weight, her great arse covering his chest then moving up to cover his face, to take all his breathing inside her and his right hand was pulling the coarse nightshirt up over his miserable body and he gasped and shuddered with the sudden, exhausting relief.

Brother James felt there was a black hole in his head, and

a wave of despair and hopelessness hurt him into tears. He sobbed into the pillow, careless of the wetness, forgetting the heat of the bed, the coarseness of the shirt, the thin mattress under him, and he cursed himself and the world and he cursed the God that had created him and womankind and the terrible struggle that went on between man and woman in this world, in his head. Then he wept the more; halfway through a sincere, groaning act of contrition, Brother James A. Dukes fell into a gracefilled and restoring sleep.

*　*　*

Juniper had to admit it, Sarah was no great cook. He did, however, greatly enjoy the meal. Partly because of the wine they drank, partly because of the Black Forest Gateau he had brought along with him. Sarah lived on the far side of the city, in Templeogue, in a semi-detached, and she told him that on a clear day you could see the Dublin mountains close by, and at night sometimes the lovely gashes of flames from the gorse on fire. It was afternoon when they sat in the lounge of her house; again smog and fog covered the city in a smelly blanket, the way an island can be lost in a fug of enchantment. She worked about the fireplace and would not let him help; he was her guest, and guests must enjoy all the hospitality she could offer. She laughed as she lit the fire and he saw an area of her lower back peep out between her jeans and blouse as she stooped over the fireplace; he swallowed hard; he must not muck this one up.

It was almost eleven o'clock before he decided he should make a move for home. They had not touched during the afternoon, Juniper feeling proud of himself, his control, the way he was allowing things to take their course. She had a half day on Wednesday, so did he; would she come to Malahide in the afternoon and he would do a meal, they could go to the pictures in town, or perhaps to a play? Of course, she would love to.

The smog was almost impenetrable. The wine was finished, the brandy bottle empty. The prospect of driving across the city and out to the suburbs on the far side was distressing. It was Sarah who suggested he stay the night and go straight to work after breakfast the following morning. It was too dangerous to drive ... she would never forgive herself if ... and the police might be out, checking ...

Sarah went upstairs to prepare a bed in the spare room. When she came down she held a floral nightdress in her hand. He heard her lovely, waterfall laughter.

'You can wear this tonight, there's nobody going to see you.'

So Juniper found himself in a cold bed in a woman's nightdress in a strange house. He felt certain he was rapidly falling in love with the young woman in the next room. He found himself unable to sleep. It was cold in the bed and the air was cold. He got up and put on his shirt and socks over the nightdress. Still no good. There was a knock and Sarah, in nightdress, raven hair falling about her face, her shoulders, smiling broadly, asked him if he could sleep, apologising for the coldness and then .... suggesting he come in with her, to her double bed where she had an electric blanket!

Juniper walked stiff as an ironing board into her room; his hairy legs showed under the nightdress; his socks embarrassed him, and he quickly slipped them off. He got into the bed beside her and she turned from him with a warm 'Goodnight James,' and doused the light. There were perhaps two inches between them; Juniper lay flat on his back, hardly daring to breathe; he could not believe this situation; so near, so lovely, so sexually attractive, but he could not, he would not, move. He lay, pretending to breathe regularly and easily; she lay quietly, her back to him, the bed was warm, this could be paradise, here he could build an everlasting city ...

There was a dull orange light on the curtains from the

street outside; Juniper imagined the smog, like those old movies he had seen of London, where werewolves prowled in search of solitary women to devour them. He did not care now if he spent the entire night awake; indeed it would be a waste to sleep. In gratitude he lay, warm and happy, the woman he loved and whose body he yearned for, whose spirit he craved to know and love, lying beside him; perhaps she was sleeping, innocent, pure, trusting in the goodness and integrity of her guest.

At one stage during the night he found he had dozed and had turned his back to her; his buttocks were pressed to hers and gently, but quickly, he eased himself away; he must not, he would not, muck this one up. Later still, when he had slept more deeply, he woke suddenly to find her breasts against his back, her arm thrown lightly over his chest. Again he lay stiff as a board, not daring to stir lest she wake and think him forward, only interested in taking advantage of an innocent girl. The night passed in an ecstacy of tension and delight, of hope and dread, of drifting towards sleep and of breaking sharply to watchfulness. Sarah slept on, breathing easily, a wonder to him, a brave, new world ...

† † †

Brother Sebastian Hone was one of the young men who had joined the novitiate at the same time as Brother James A. Dukes. Sebastian had a sweet face, he was tall and well-formed. He was the same age as James and after some considerable time of close proximity to each other James found himself falling in love with Brother Sebastian. He watched him, dimly aware of a sensation of particular fondness growing inside. He gazed at him, surreptitiously, taken by his features, anxious to be in his company.

The Brothers were not allowed to choose their company; on the way to the recreation yard after midday meal, one had to take the recreation period with the first two Brothers who came out the yard door. There was a field, around it a cinder track; here the postulants walked, anti-clockwise, round and round the track, until the time was up. They spoke together, elevating conversations at all times. Now and again James noticed he was holding back, or speeding up, in order to reach the yard door at the same time as Brother Sebastian; he was jovial and talkative in his company; he was sullen and angry when they were not together. Soon he found himself beginning to resent Sebastian for not trying to be in James's company; he was irked with any Brother who seemed to be getting on well with Sebastian. He sat in the library, thinking often of the young Brother, gazing dreamily at the back of his head.

One day, when Brother James was on laundry duty, he had to go into the Brothers' cells to collect the soiled linen. When he was in Sebastian's cell he was unable to resist the impulse to bury his face in the linen, hoping to inhale his scent. Up to that moment James had not felt there was anything strange or reprehensible in this infatuation; he had no reason to suspect this particular friendship could be other than normal and natural. Now he knew it had become a burden, interrupting his thoughts, diverting his concentration from God. James was suffering. His head buried in the scent of the absent Brother, he was slithering down a path with a cliff-fall at its end.

For some time he went in the opposite direction, avoiding all contact with Brother Sebastian. This was not easy, living as they did in the same house, eating at the same table, studying in the same corner of the library. James quickly realised that trying to avoid the Brother actually brought him much more often into his thoughts and actions. He suffered the more, offering up his pain for the lost and lonely of this world.

On a wet afternoon Brother James was passing ten minutes

of idleness before Vespers in the tiny waiting-room near the Monks' quarters. He picked up and glanced through a copy of the *National Geographic* magazine. As he flicked across the pages an article with its accompanying photographs struck him a sharp blow; it pictured a tribe somewhere in the Amazon Basin, men and women and children in the simplicity of complete nakedness. James lingered longer than he ought over some of the pictures. There were women stooping over pots or feeding their young, there were men with weapons, who stood gazing out at the reader, there was one lovely woman smiling out at James while she straddled a pony. His stomach flared into fire as he gazed at her and a surge of life came from beneath his habit. He knew an overwhelming stress of mind and body as he looked into those frank eyes and followed the grace of the naked body. He left the room as quickly as he could.

Brother James, agitated, walked down the corridor, his long habit swishing about his legs; he ran up the stone staircase, gathering the habit about his waist; he hurried along the first floor corridor, through a door into the chaplain's quarters where everything smelt of waxed celibacy. He knocked on Father MacSeamus's door and prayed to God that the green light would come on before his courage failed. The light shone; God was waiting.

Father MacSeamus was reading by a small desk-light; the room was dim and musty in the early evening, bachelor-cluttered, a coat thrown on the end of a half-made bed, a pair of muddy shoes left on the window-sill.

'Father, I'd like to confess, now, at once. Please.'

'OK, Brother James, just sit down over there and let me put on my stole. Now, let's hear what crimes you've been at along the cloisters.'

Father MacSeamus took out his purple stole, kissed it and put it about his neck, carefully settling the tasselled ends so that they were hanging evenly on either side of his chest. This short, intense ritual threw a gloomy seriousness about the room. The priest blessed himself, murmuring words, laid his left elbow on his left knee, buried his forehead in his left hand, his right hand lying idly on his right knee, ready for dispensing absolution.

'Bless me, Father, for I have sinned ... ' and James told him about the magazine, about the pictures, about his erection.

'Well now, Brother James, did you enter the room looking for such pictures?'

'Oh no, Father, I was just idling for a few moments, and I came across them, by accident ... '

'And you lingered over them, you were excited by them?'

'Yes, Father.'

'And you feel you lingered over them a bit too long?'

'Yes, Father.'

'And did you take pleasure in this excitement? Did you yield, consciously and deliberately so you could prolong this excitement?'

'Well, no Father, I don't think you could say that.'

'When you realised you were getting an erection did you leave the pictures down at once?'

'Yes, Father.'

'Very good. And tell me now, Brother James, did you touch yourself at all during this incident?'

'Oh no, Father, no indeed, I did not.'

'Well now, Brother James, no harm done, no harm done. Isn't it natural for a young healthy man like yourself to be disturbed by pictures of naked women? Between a man and a woman, Brother James, there is something sacred, something that is perhaps the richest source of dignity and value in human living, something at the same time that is the source of man's deepest need and his most powerful temptation. That is as it ought to be. If God above has given mankind something so precious as human love, then I think the price we have to pay in terms of need and longing is a fair one. All of that is very good and beautiful and holy; when you join the Brothers nothing of that changes within you, the same needs and instincts will remain. You're a man, Brother James, you'll always be a man, you'll always find yourself attracted to women, believe me. But now you have offered up to God all that pleasure and fulfilment, to gain a higher love and a higher fulfilment. You are putting away this gift somewhere in the recesses of your life, hoping for a greater gift. As long as you don't set out to look for this kind of stimulation, as long as you do not willingly give into it if it does occur, then you are gaining all the time in the power to make that love turn towards God himself, and that, James, is an unbelievable wonder, to love and to be loved by God, and by his Most Blessed Mother. You would be a strange class of a fellow wouldn't you if you weren't attracted by such a picture?'

Father MacSeamus paused. Brother James remained silent.

'Was there anything else, Brother James?'

'No, Father, not really. I think you have answered my problems. And I'm very grateful. Thank you Father.'

'Praise God in his holy place, Brother James, praise God.'

Brother James left the room in deeper worry than when he had entered. Had he now compounded his crimes by making a bad confession?

That night, in the library, he was reading the Everyman Edition of the Poems of Pope. All at once the dull, monotonous rhythms and language of Alexander Pope began to scream at him from the page. The opening of 'Eloïse to Abelard':

> *In these deep solitudes and awful cells,*
> *Where heavenly-pensive Contemplation dwells,*
> *And ever-musing Melancholy reigns,*
> *What means this tumult in a Vestal's veins?*
> *Why rove my thoughts beyond this last retreat?*
> *Why feels my heart its long-forgotten heat?*

Apart from the rhetorical questioning, the stiff couplets, the capital letters, his tussling with the word 'Vestal', Brother James was stricken.

> *Hide it, my heart, within that close disguise,*
> *Where, mix'd with God's, his loved idea lies ...*

And then:

> *Canst thou forget what tears that moment fell,*
> *When warm in youth I bade the world farewell?*
> *As with cold lips I kiss'd the sacred veil,*
> *The shrines all trembled, and the lamps grew pale;*
> *Heaven scarce believed the conquest it survey'd*
> *And saints with wonder heard the vows I made.*
> *Yet then, to those dread altars as I drew,*
> *Not on the cross my eyes were fix'd, but you;*
> *Not grace, or zeal, love only was my call;*
> *And if I lose thy love, I lose my all.*
> *Come! with thy looks, thy words, relieve my woe;*
> *Those still at least are left thee to bestow.*

Brother James went through the poem, underlining passages in soft pencil, taking care to avoid the owl eyes of Brother Boniface, librarian. Then he scribbled a note: 'Please read; and meet me at 5.15pm. in the Small Reading-Room. James.' Then, without allowing himself any hesitation, he put the note inside the book, at the correct page, and walked up to where Brother Sebastian was reading at his desk.

* * *

Sarah arrived on Wednesday, earlier than Juniper had anticipated. She wore tight denim jeans and a pink wool sweater. He was in the boat, trying to firm up part of the floorboards where there seemed to be cracks. He called her in to the boat and she sat on the bunk behind him. He had a bottle of wine waiting; he poured them out a glassfull each.

'I just want to paint over these boards on the floor, or the deck, or whatever it is; then I'm going to put in another bunk on this side.'

'Another bunk? Why another bunk?'

'Well, at some stage it may be needed. I really don't want to spend the rest of my days alone, you know. Maybe somebody might join up with me sometime, so I'll need another bunk.'

She laughed, and he got down on the floor quickly with the brush and varnish. He was lying along the floor of the cabin, reaching for some awkward parts when, without warning, she stood up and, laughing, stepped across him; then she sat down on the small of his back, straddling him, and he gasped with joy as he took her weight and felt the fullness of her buttocks against him.

Her soft and musical laughter sent shocks of delight through him.

'Lift up your feet,' she said, 'and I'll help you with your painting.'

She began taking off his shoes and socks; then from her handbag she took nail varnish and began to paint his toenails a bright red. Juniper slowed down at his work and wished that he had two hundred toes for her to work on. She moved around gently on his back, settling herself on him, shifting to get more easily at his toes. When she had finished she lifted herself above him, turned and squatted down on his back again.

'Now,' she said, 'turn over and see the fine job I've done.'

She lifted herself a little, allowing him to turn over on his back; then she sat down again, her weight on his stomach and chest taking his breath from him. He gazed past her at his toes and laughed contentedly. He wished they could stay like this forever.

'I think I'd like to die here,' he ventured.

She laughed again, then began to move on him, rhythmically rolling her body, a movement that sent waves of pleasure through him.

'Why wouldn't *you* come with me to Italy?'

'And give up my job and all my prospects for a pensioned future? To sail with Popeye on the seas of the world?' She was chuckling. 'There's nothing I'd like more, but I don't think I'd have the courage for it.'

He began to talk again of his plans. The money he'd have saved. The prospects for getting a teaching position in Italy. There were no limits to his hopes. They could end up in Tahiti. Or in Iceland. Or anywhere in the world. She reached to the table and poured herself another glass of wine. She sat quietly on him now; she was serious.

'It's a crazy scheme, and it might just work. For you. I don't know if there is a future in it. For me.'

He raised himself on one elbow, took a sip of his wine, and sank down under her again.

'And there could be accidents. What if this old tub of yours hits a rock? or the engine gives out? Or a ship runs into you in the darkness? What if you're caught in a gale off Cape Horn, then where would you be?'

'I'm investing in a good outboard engine,' he said, 'to be fitted onto the back just in case of an emergency. I'll always stay close to the coast. I don't intend to budge if there's the remotest possibility of bad weather.'

She was silent, sipping her wine, gazing down at him. For both of them, in that garage, suburbia ticking away beyond the door, the world was small and warm and full of possibilities. Juniper had never known such bliss as he tried to sense with his body every inch of her as she pressed down on his chest. He gazed up at her, into her thoughtful face, the lips shining now with the moisture of the wine. Let us build here two tabernacles ...

† † †

The Small Reading-Room was the room where Brother James had his encounter with the naked Amazonian woman. He found it fitting that he should situate the beginning of his redemption in that same room. A small room, the rest of the violent, demanding world ticking away just outside its walls, its door.

Brother James opened the door at ten minutes after the hour. As his hand closed on the knob of the door a thought came to him; what if Sebastian were to announce an answering, overwhelming passion of his own for Brother James? then what? The thought came like a punch to the stomach; where would they go from there? would they become lovers? in a monastery? and what on earth would that involve? Oh God, please let him not come at all ...

Brother Ludovic Casey was in the Small Reading-Room; he was sitting at the table, immersed in a volume of 'Studies'. Taking notes. He glanced up at Brother James, nodded, and went back to his reading. Ludovic the Terrible, some of the more earthy Brothers called him; he was lanky, yellow-haired, a monk who exhibited none of the virtues required by the Rules and Constitution, nor any of those urged on the Brothers for the development of their souls. He was built on the model of Dickens's Uriah Heep: squirmish, outspoken, ugly, gangly, his habit hanging about his frame like a dressing-gown on a patient who had entered hospital at fifteen stone and now walked the corridors at eight stone ten.

The nature of Brother James's impending communion was such that the presence of a third party was out of the question. James fiddled with the magazine rack for a moment, begging Divine Intervention. Then he sat at the table opposite Ludovic whose telephone-pole legs, crossed at the ankles, reached under the table and protruded on James's side. James uncapped a bottle of black ink, took out his pen and began to unscrew it; suddenly he lurched, and the ink went tumbling onto the shoes, socks and trouser legs of Reverend Brother

Ludovic Casey — and onto the polished parquet floor.

'Oh, Brother Ludovic, I'm sorry, forgive me, oh how clumsy of me!'

Ludovic jumped up and watched the ink settle gently into his clothes. 'You're a right yearning shit-hawk, Brother James!' said the saint, risking his immortal soul by breaking several of the rules at once. 'Look at my shoes, my socks, even my trousers. God but you're a crass twit surely!'

Ludovic left the reading-room to the victor. James took out a handkerchief and got to work on the floor. There was a dark stain but by dint of spitting on the floor and mopping with one of his own socks, he got it comparatively clean. He was sweating, but he had succeeded. As he looked at the memory of the black stain he knew that all of this manoeuvering had already freed him of Brother Sebastian. Now he would merely ask him if he had liked the poem, and that would be that. Brother James chuckled to himself; poor Brother Ludovic had unwittingly become the catalyst for Brother James's fears; the stain would soon fade, James thought, as would his own intense feeling. At five twenty-five Brother Sebastian had not turned up. At five forty the bell would ring for Vespers.

He sat down at the table and flicked through a copy of the *Far East*. He laughed at himself now, and glanced over at the offending copy of the *National Geographic*. At precisely five thirty-nine the door opened. Brother James jumped to his feet. It was Ludovic, and James sat down again, exhausted, at the table. He was aware that, if it had been Sebastian, he would have felt embarrassed and abashed at the episode he had gone through. He remembered the young Amazonian beauty astride her horse; even the memory of her picture stirred him; he felt now that something small, natural and disposable had grown like a mushroom in the darkness within him and had exploded in a puff of smoke. As the bell for Vespers rang he stood up, reached over his hand to

Brother Ludovic and said, 'Dear confrère, I thank you from
the bottom of my heart.'

Ludovic's mouth was a thin line of anger and annoyance.

* * *

During the mid-term break Juniper headed off on a short
holiday to Rome. He wandered breathlessly about that city
and one day took the bus out along the Autostrada del Sole,
turning off after some time, heading up the Flaminia Way. At
last, after so many, many years, Assisi became visible, a small
town rising over the sunflower plains of Umbria, still far off
in the haze of a shimmering afternoon. It was as if he were
coming home. The bus approached slowly; there were acres
of sunflowers, watching the sky like a huge congregation of
suffering souls who had turned to Francis for ease and
comfort on the long, potholed road towards death.

The bus climbed the hill into the town. Juniper headed at
once through the dusty streets to the Basilica of St Francis
where he moved about, hushed and prayerful. The walls
were covered with frescoes and Juniper followed them
through to see if he could discover the original, the great and
holy Saint, Juniper, companion to Francis himself. He could
not distinguish one figure from the other. In the crypt he knelt
before the stone sarcophagus that contained the uncorrupted
body of the great Saint Francis. There were chains fastening
it against the curious, and it was locked away far from the
reach of tourist or penitent.

He wandered about the town, stunned at all the sacred
objects that were on sale, searching, through books and
medals and holy pictures, for some mention of his namesake.
He read of Bernard, Elias, Leo, Masseo, there were tales of
the wolf of Gubbio, pictures of the mountain of the Seraph,
of the wondrous Stigmata offered to Francis; but nowhere
could he find mention of Juniper, the little saint, the foolish,

humble one, the comedian.

At one stage he drew in among a crowd of American tourists who were being guided around the town. A young Italian woman was the guide; Juniper loved the colour of her skin, the bright happiness on her face, the rich brown colour of her eyes. She spoke with authority on all things Franciscan and at one stage, hesitantly, attempting a slight American drawl, he asked her: 'Can you tell us anything of Brother Juniper?'

The young woman smiled and said it was now generally believed that Brother Juniper did not, in fact, exist. He was an amalgam of several of the more simple-minded followers of Francis who became especially fervent in the presence of the Saint. Once, she said, a madman had escaped from a house near Assisi and had gone to Rome, telling everyone he had been sent by Francis and would work wonders for them all. Then, a large crowd around him, he raised his arms towards heaven and called on God to send down a flight of doves with coins for all the pilgrims gathered round. Nothing happened. The crowd jeered and hooted. He knelt before them and offered his body to be humiliated. Several of them beat him with their staffs and threw stones at him. He was knocked unconscious under all the blows and was carried to a house by a kindly woman who took him to be one of the great, suffering saints. When he was well again she sent him by carriage to Assisi where he was immediately brought back into the madhouse. The legend grew that this person was one Juniper who had come deliberately to suffer humiliation for the glory of God. Nowhere, the woman told him, in all the historical records was there anything to prove Juniper ever existed, no tomb, no relics, Juniper was a dream, a hope, a wisp, a breath.

* * *

When he came home, Juniper and Sarah met on a damp, mizzling afternoon. They went for a drive along the estuary of the River Boyne. Near the mouth of the river a steep slope led down from an old boathouse into the water; it was here, Juniper told her, he would launch the 'Sarah'. There was a stench of rotting things about them, a miasma, hanging over the tidal shores of the estuary. Mussel boats lay above the water mark, faces down, as if they had been spewed out like corpses from the river. Further downriver the channel opened out into the Irish Sea.

They stood for a short while in the cold air near the river; the stones were covered in a green slime; Sarah shivered; there was a sadness in her face, a quietness about her Juniper could not touch. A sudden impulse made him reach out his arm to hold her. Then he drew it back quickly, afraid to do the slightest thing to destroy what may have been growing between them.

They went into the pub at Mornington, a dark-wood pub and general store where a gas fire sputtered and two young men were playing darts. It gave Juniper a surge of pride to hold Sarah's elbow and lead her to a bench near a window, proprietorially asking her what she would like to drink. The dart players paused to watch them for a moment, then they resumed their game. As he stood at the bar and ordered two gin and tonics Juniper made up his mind that today he would make a real attempt to kiss her. At once he grew more wary, watching every move she made, every sigh or smile or movement towards or away from him. When she asked for a packet of crisps his heart sagged; he would not take any himself, thinking of his breath, how he must keep it pure and unsullied for the day.

'Are you all right?' he asked her.

'Yes, fine, just a little chilled, I think.'

They followed the contours of the river for some miles inland, the heater on the car turned up full, the windows

dimmed from their breathing. The road was slippery with
wet leaves; there was a heaviness and a dead rusty colour
on all the trees. Sarah's mood responded to the day and
Juniper's yearning began to hurt him deeply. They turned
towards the great burial mounds of the Boyne Valley.

He parked the car outside the cairn of Dowth. They paid
at the turnstile and walked along muddy ground to the
entrance. They had to stoop and clamber with difficulty
down a narrow, low passage into the earth, down, like
animals burrowing. Above them the great mound stood,
heavy, wet and still. There were dim lights and Juniper went
ahead, ready to hold her should she slip. Their voices echoed
disconcertingly in the deep underearth.

At last they could stand up again in the main chamber.
This too was lit dimly; the floor was hard and smooth from
many visitors, the air dry, they knew they were intruders in
a tomb.

'How would you care to be buried with my family?' he
hazarded as a half jest. She grinned at him. The chamber was
small, they were aware of the tons of rock and clay above
their heads, of all the many centuries of dying and decay
about them. They stood close together, looking round with
caution as if loud voices might bring the place down on top
of them.

She shuddered, with cold, with whatever thoughts were
going through her mind.

'Will we go?' he suggested.

She looked up into his face and there was a sadness in her
eyes that cowed him. There was tenderness, too, and she
caught his hands suddenly, where he held them by his sides,
lifted her face towards him and kissed him on the mouth, a
quick kiss that sent warmth through him. He tried to respond
but she had drawn back again and was turning towards the
passageway out of the tomb. The scent of crisps and the
juniper scent of gin had given her breath a sourness he

thought suited to the place they were in.

Then she was stooping forward in the passageway, start-ing the ascent back up the wet, earthy slope to the light. Juniper came behind her. He was aflame after her kiss and now her lovely full buttocks were there before him as she crouched to get back to the day. Her jeans were of faded denim, outlining her body beautifully. She slipped, flopped onto her knees and slid back against him. He reached forward and caught her; his hands were round her buttocks, restrain-ing her, and he lost himself at once, after all those long, tortured years he grasped her body and buried his face against her, kissing her buttocks in a helpless frenzy, letting out small cries like a hurt animal. She did not resist, allowing her body to sway back against him; his frenzy grew. Then she turned towards him and she was frenzied, too, pushing him back into the chamber.

She was opening her jeans and calling to him, 'now, now, now,' then she was on the earth and he was fumbling on top of her, opening his trousers, trying with desperation to redeem the moment. She grew impatient, grabbing him and pulling him down onto her, thrusting her tongue into his mouth, trying to draw his body into hers. He came almost at once, against her, and she screamed at him, and he was helpless, shaken, and at a loss.

She pushed him away from her and got up, fastening her jeans. Her clothes were darkened by the clay and she asked him to rub it off; he took tissues from her bag and rubbed her jeans and jacket as best he could; then she was climbing quickly up the passageway ahead of him. The tears were flowing down his face as he followed her and his efforts to wipe them away drew long black smudges over his cheeks and forehead. He emerged from the earth into a darkening day, she had hurried to the car before he could catch her up.

'Take me home quickly now, please, I'm very cold.'

Several days passed before he had the courage to phone

her. She was quiet and considerate on the phone but told him
she had met another man, a younger one, and had hoped to
tell Juniper about it during their day along the Boyne. She
was sorry. She was grateful to him for the lovely time they
had together. No it was nothing to do with Dowth, nothing
at all. She knew he'd find somebody else and be happy. Soon.
Thank you again. And good luck with all your plans. I'm very
sorry. Goodbye, Juniper.

That day he drove to the marina and bought an expensive
outboard engine. He decided he would take the boat for a
trial run on the Boyne as soon as possible. As soon as possible
he would collect what was due to him and he would leave.
He would head for warmer shores. He would run away. For
ever.

† † †

Towards the end of the first year Brother James A. Dukes was
put in charge of the bicycles. Many of the Brothers cycled
daily into the city colleges. There were twenty-five bicycles
in the shed, each having a number painted on in white, glossy
figures, from one to twenty-five. The numbers were allocated
in order of superiority; bike one was a new bike, a Raleigh
with three-speed gears; after number ten there were no more
gears; number twenty was a lady's bike, helping the Brother
who was given it to grow in humility and to develop his leg
muscles to keep up with the others. Bikes twenty-three,
twenty-four and twenty-five were antiquities of the countryside, uncertain in their parts, bent, buckled and bewildered.

Brother Matthew Havers, second year novice, student
teacher, middle-of-the-road saint, was allocated bike sixteen.
Early in May Brother Matthew, scarcely nineteen years of
age, came off bike sixteen on a straight road and was crushed
to death by a passing lorry.

Many of the Brothers were in tears during the next several

days. Matthew was to be buried in the small graveyard beyond the monastery playing fields. The Havers family agreed. The mourning days began.

All flesh shall come to you, oh God, all flesh shall come to you where you wait enthroned in the new Jerusalem. Brother James watched and listened during the awesome Solemn High Mass. His whole body was alert as any fox who has heard in the distance a faint echo of the hounds and horn. The love affair he was involved in was being put to the test; the solemnity, the chanting, the slow determined rituals of incense, prayer and movement, could all of this, and all the centuries, and all the history be merely an empty show, without substance? Matthew lay broken and dead. James thought of the empty space in the bicycle stand, like a gap broken in a wall, like a hole left in the heart.

The day advanced slowly towards release. There was a silent procession from the Chapel on that grey forenoon, down across the gravel walk to a tiny graveyard. In the Chapel tower the bell tolled, every thirty seconds, slow, insistent, chilling. The novices and Brothers and priests and the Havers family, formed a slow, sad line across the grounds, surplices and soutanes caught and mocked by the breeze. Brother Matthew was lowered into his narrow bed. May flights of angels bear thee into Paradise. The priest sprinkled water and a shovelful of clay.

A light rain was falling as the Brothers made their way back to the monastery. Each was alone again, each soul flung back, solitary and separate, into his particular cell. Brother James was deeply sad and hurt. In the afternoon he walked away alone, breaking one of the rules, into the quiet of the gardens and shrubbery along the front avenue. Now the sun had come out again, weak and watery, but there. Brother Rufino Collins was sitting on a bench under a high, fuchsia hedge. James paused to watch.

Rufino must have been ninety years old. He lived now in

the Blue House, an old mansion reserved for the years of retirement. James had often seen him wandering close to the edge of the novices' grounds, heavy on his stick, leaning over a railing and dropping pebbles into a stream. Rufino had a reputation for holiness; he was credited with opening the order's first school in South-West-Africa. Brother James longed to speak to him, to talk to him of Matthew, of the order, of God...

He watched the old man now, sitting there, his habit frayed and heavy on him, the stick idle between his knees. He was dozing, his head fallen low onto his chest. James wondered if a man can ever succeed, even after so many years of dedication, in overcoming or even quelling the isolation that is his lot. Not loneliness, he thought, not even isolation, something more, unnameable because intolerable. He remembered that awful hole in the graveyard where Matthew, nineteen years of age, now lay. Rufino must be aware that the next hole would probably be for him. Is it possible? to overcome, before death, that one-being-ness, separation from all others and from the world; the coffin always there, forbidding warm contact with another; to find the understanding of even one other person who could anticipate your needs without despising you for them, who could participate in your memories, listen to the inanities of which you are capable without excoriating you for them; someone who cares if your body hurts, if your mind chills; someone who answers the questions you haven't asked; someone who asks the questions you want to answer; someone who has touched their vulnerability to yours. Someone who loves you. Whom you love.

Rufino rose, shakily. James watched the old man move in amongst the fuchsia bushes, pick a few of the scarlet flowers and squeeze the juice from them onto his palm. He sneezed, and a fit of coughing brought him, heavy and stooped over his stick, back towards the house. But it was enough for

James, watching from beyond the hedge. He was at home again, and remembering Sarah, little Sarah Higgins. When he was small she had always called him Jimmy and when she said the name it sounded precious on her lips. She would shake her head and laugh, her curls bouncing carelessly and her bright blue eyes sparkling. Those were the years when young boys were supposed to hold young girls in contempt; Jimmy Dukes had, even then, ached to be in her company. Then came that day they had sheltered together in the tumbledown gate lodge of an old estate, he and she, alone. What age was he then? twelve, perhaps, and she, perhaps the same. After the shower the sun had shone with fresh brilliance and the fuchsia leaves gleamed and glistened, their hanging flowers taking on a wet, rich scarlet hue that glowed like lights in a green darkness. Jimmy picked several of them and squeezed the honey onto the back of his wrist, big, shining drops of nectar. He had called eagerly to her to come and see. He held out his wrist towards her. She came, laughing, tossing her curls, and bent down her mouth to his wrist and licked the honey from his flesh. Then she hopped away from him, laughing, looking back towards him. His hand burned, his body gathered itself about the wrist so that for some minutes he could not stir.

Had Rufino remembered something like that? Or had he grown immune to his selfhood by a din of prayers, teaching and missionary zeal? Did the natural withering of the mind, this dithering, dozing existence he was now living, did all of that blur real need within his soul? James could not ask. How could he? The young Brother turned to the stone Madonna high above the monastery walk and gazed into those stone eyes. Mary, Virgin, Mother of Dolours, the woman whose vulnerability towards creation was so total that from it came the most perfect creature of us all. Gate of Heaven. Comforter of the Afflicted. Lover? The last word seemed reprehensible and he tried to put it away. He could not. Only the image of the young girl, Sarah, would come to him. James knelt before the grotto, and cried hot, scalding tears before the stone Madonna. Rufino continued his halting walk towards the door and disappeared inside. Waiting.

And then, at last, after so many years, the great day for the young Brothers finally dawned; they were to make their final vows, amid all the pomp and ritual of a Great High Mass. James A. Dukes was to lie, with others, on the marble shore of the altar steps, prostrate as a cast-up body would have been, waiting for the touch that would bring him, for eternity, into the community of God's chosen ones. He had decided on the name he would take — *Juniper* — the lowly one, the humble, uncertain one, the close friend of Francis.

Instead, while the other Brothers were singing Lauds in the chapel, James A. Dukes stood at the bus stop outside the monastery walls. They had given him enough money to buy himself a suit of clothes, (turd-brown, double-breasted, pin-striped) a shirt and tie, new shoes. In his hand he held what was left to him after his voyage across those years, a paper bag with some underclothes, socks, a large, brass crucifix.

The bus came and he clambered aboard, making his way self-consciously along the aisle between half-empty rows of mid-morning shoppers. The bus pulled away. He gazed back at the receding gates and shuddered. He had come so close, so close ...

At the next stop a young woman got on the bus and stopped to pay the driver. James watched her; she was dressed in jeans and blouse and was very pretty. James looked away, quickly, a feeling of guilt striking him. Then, very deliberately, he looked back and followed the movements of her body as she came down the aisle and climbed to the upper deck. James smiled to himself, sat back and thought, 'After all, it is, at last, the end of the middle ages.'

* * *

It was Saturday, December; the air was chilled through, the sky grey, gale force winds forecast for late evening. Not, perhaps, the very best day for the trial. But his heart was so dulled that he knew he could easily sink into a mood from which he might never emerge if he did not take this step, if only to prove the possibility of his voyage really did exist.

He borrowed a car with a towbar. 'Sarah' was not quite finished but all that was left was cosmetic work. He had run the motor a few times and it had purred sweetly. He attached the new outboard engine to the stern. Now he must try the water. He had dressed for the part: waders, aran sweater, heavy coat, oilskins folded up and stowed in the cabin. He had a cap he knew looked rakish, a gift from Diamond offered with a half-envious laugh. He took the coast road and was driving through Laytown shortly after one o'clock. In the village the playground was deserted, the swings and slides wet, the seaside town abandoned for the winter. There were lights on already in some of the houses and in the pub.

He took the sharp turn to the left and there, in front of him, was the Irish Sea! calm and dark and waiting. He stopped the car with its precious trailer and got out. He sauntered about car and boat, pretending to be making sure that everything was in order. He savoured the moment, looking at 'Sarah' with love, then turning towards the sea, the horizon, the few gulls trying to feed along the shore.

He got to the slipway at one thirty. He reversed boat and car carefully down to the river; the towbar was in the water before he braked fully, the back wheels of the car almost touching the fast-flowing waters of the river Boyne. He made sure the anchor was safely caught between rocks at the slipway's edge; he loosened the boat from the towbar and to his absolute delight and some amazement 'Sarah' was afloat. He took the car away from the river and parked it among the dunes. Then he climbed aboard.

'Sarah' was straining hard against the anchor rope, the

current strong even here at the edge of the river. The tide was half-way out, the whole thrust of the river offered a challenge to any boat attempting to move upriver. This was precisely the test he had planned, for 'Sarah' and for himself. He would make his way upriver as far as Drogheda, go under the bridges in the town and out into the calmer waters beyond. Here he could turn and let the force of the ebbing tide bring him back to his starting point.

He tried the engine; it caught at once. He throttled gently and she responded; he could hear the delightful sound of the propellor churning the water behind him, he sensed the slight thrust forward of the boat. He drew in the anchor, chucking it carefully from among the rocks and immediately tide and current took the boat downriver. He turned her easily and faced upriver, the engine beginning to roar with the effort. He could sense the power as she began to thrust forward, the shuddering of the boards as she realised she was alive. He made slow but steady progress against the currents; she responded to the slightest touch on the throttle; he whooped with joy and kissed the wheel between his hands. The wind was gusting, there was a mist of rain on the windscreen, but he was in control.

He noticed that the instruments on the panel in front of him did not seem to be functioning; he had no idea what speed he was making. These, too, were reasons for a trial run at this stage; it would be easy to rectify such small details, it would be easy, too, to install the radio he would buy himself for Christmas. Now he was moving slowly towards the great curve in the river Boyne where it widens between the mud-flats and then straightens out again in the run towards Drogheda. He kept her out of the main rush of the currents, closer to the left bank. He eased the wheel into the long curve and the engine gave a first, gasping splutter. He glanced at the instruments but they told him nothing. He knew he had filled the engine with the correct fuel. He touched the starter and the engine roared again; the moment passed.

Once again 'Sarah' was responding with ease. The wind was coming from starboard and bringing the rain more directly in on the deck; but his sense of exhilaration persisted. A cormorant passed him, heading upriver low over the surface of the water and he could see its baleful eye turned towards him as it passed, the sheen of its black feathers, the way the tips of the wings skimmed the water on each down beat. He laughed out loud.

Again the engine stuttered, and stalled. There was a sudden, awful silence. He could hear the rush of the water like a low, determined growl all about him. 'Sarah' slewed around and the bows were at once facing downriver again. He touched the starter several times, each time with mounting desperation. He held the starter down, the engine coughed once more; there was a strange, unpleasant click, and the starting trigger came away in his hand. The boat was moving silently and swiftly downriver, following the flow of the current, taking the great curve with grace. He did not panic. He moved to the stern, lowered the outboard engine and, with a heartfelt prayer, pulled on the starting chord. It took three anguished tugs before it caught, roared and jerked the boat forward. He breathed a prayer of gratitude and took hold of the rudder. He would ease 'Sarah' back to the slipway, abandon the test and see to the small, rusting parts of the panel.

By now the slipway had been passed and he tried to bring 'Sarah' about to face back, at an angle, to the shore. The boat juddered against the ever strengthening current. The outboard was at full throttle, 'Sarah' shuddered suddenly, there was a loud, splintering noise and the engine, with the whole stern panel to which it was bolted, disappeared into the turmoil of the river.

Silence descended once more. Only the rushing noise of the waters against the yielding hull could be heard, the rain that was beginning to fall heavily, the wails of a rising wind. It was growing dark; soon even the lights of Mornington village would be invisible behind the rains and darkness. The boat was moving out towards the estuary mouth, towards the open sea. He watched the restraining boulders at the mouth of the river, he could just make out the deserted beach, a faint yellow thread in the distance.

For some reason he thought of that dark, sad day when he had found himself beached on the strange shore of the novitiate, when he had watched his grandmother sitting lost and alone; he could remember her scent, her words — 'Father James. Father James Dukes. I'm so very, very proud of you.' He remembered how the tears had smudged the thick powders on her old face. Nanna.

The guiding lights at the harbour mouth were flashing, accentuating the emptiness and the silence he felt within him. He was drifting rapidly, out and out and out. Soon it was wholly dark, the flashing of the lights barely visible in the distance. He went into the cabin and closed the hatch behind him. He lay down on the bunk and closed his eyes. The storm was increasing moment by moment; 'Sarah' bucked and pitched sickeningly.

*   †   *   †   *